ABOUT THIS BOOK

MISCHIEVOUS MEG
by Astrid Lindgren
Pictures by Janina Domanska

Alva is sure Meg will stay out of trouble when she promises to picnic close by the house. But Alva never expects that Meg will picnic *on* the house, serving a feast for herself and her little sister, Betsy, on the roof. And what could be a better finale to the banquet than a quick flight down, though with Father's umbrella as a parachute, the flight's a lot quicker than Meg had hoped.

Things never quite turn out as Meg plans, but the surprise conclusions are half the fun when plotting mischief, Meg's favorite pastime. A year on June Hill, her family's estate by a river in Sweden, finds Meg getting into, and somehow out of, more trouble than her loving and slightly frazzled parents can imagine. From launching Betsy down the river in their mother's washtub—for a game of "Moses in the Bulrushes"—to confronting friend Albert's family ghosts in a dark cellar, Meg finds pranks to keep her family and friends amused all year long. And when a new spring arrives, since the Moses game already sank, maybe Betsy would prefer to play "Joseph in the Well"?

MISCHIEVOUS MEG

Also by Astrid Lindgren

PIPPI LONGSTOCKING

BILL BERGSON, MASTER DETECTIVE

BILL BERGSON LIVES DANGEROUSLY

MIO, MY SON

PIPPI GOES ON BOARD

PIPPI IN THE SOUTH SEAS

RASMUS AND THE VAGABOND

THE CHILDREN OF NOISY VILLAGE

HAPPY TIMES IN NOISY VILLAGE

CHRISTMAS IN NOISY VILLAGE

BILL BERGSON AND THE WHITE ROSE RESCUE

SPRINGTIME IN NOISY VILLAGE

SEACROW ISLAND

KARLSSON-ON-THE-ROOF

Mischievous Meg

ASTRID LINDGREN

Pictures by Janina Domanska
Translated by Gerry Bothmer

PUFFIN BOOKS

PUFFIN BOOKS

Viking Penguin Inc., 40 West 23rd Street, New York, New York 10010, U.S.A.
Penguin Books Ltd, Harmondsworth, Middlesex, England
Penguin Books Australia Ltd, Ringwood, Victoria, Australia
Penguin Books Canada Limited, 2801 John Street, Markham, Ontario, Canada L3R 1B4
Penguin Books (N.Z.) Ltd, 182–190 Wairau Road, Auckland 10, New Zealand

Originally published in Swedish under the title *Madicken*
by Rabén & Sjögren 1960
This English translation first published in the United States
of America by Viking Penguin Inc. 1962
Published in Puffin Books 1985
Reprinted 1985

Printed in the United States of America by
R. R. Donnelley & Sons Company, Harrisonburg, Virginia
Set in Garamond #3

Library of Congress Cataloging in Publication Data
Lindgren, Astrid, 1907–   Mischievous Meg.
Translation of: Madicken.
Originally published: New York: Viking Press, 1962.
Summary: The escapades of a nine-year-old Swedish girl and her younger sister,
as they picnic on the woodshed roof, play Moses in the bulrushes, go for a
walk on the frozen river, and celebrate Christmas.
1. Children's stories, Swedish. [1. Sweden—Fiction] I. Domanska, Janina, ill.
II. Title. PZ7.L6585Mi 1985   [Fic]   85-575   ISBN 0 14 03.1954 9

Contents

MISCHIEVOUS MEG

CHAPTER I

A Summer Day on June Hill

Meg lived in a big red house down by a river in Sweden. Her family consisted of her mother, her father, her little sister Elizabeth, a black poodle named Sasso, a kitten called Gosan, and Alva. Meg and Elizabeth had a room of their own, Alva lived in the maid's room, Sasso in his basket in the hall, and Gosan in front of the kitchen stove. Mother lived all over the house, and Father too, except when he was at his newspaper office writing, so that people in town could have something to read.

Meg's real name was Margaret, but when she was a little girl she had called herself Meggie, and although now she had grown into quite a big girl—almost ten—she was still called by a shortened form of that name: Meg. It was only when she had been naughty and was being scolded that she was called Margaret. She was called Margaret quite often. Elizabeth was called Betsy and seldom needed to be scolded, but Meg was full of rash impulses and didn't use her head, until afterward. Then she was always sorry for what she had done. She really wanted to be good and obedient, and it was a shame that things often didn't work out that way.

"That child gets her wild ideas as fast as a pig can blink," Ida would say, and that was true. Ida came out from town on Fridays to do the washing and cleaning.

One Friday, Meg was sitting on the landing at the water's edge, watching Ida rinse the laundry in the river. She was feeling very contented because she had her pockets stuffed with sweet yellow plums, and as she ate them, one after another, she kicked her bare feet in the water and sang:

> "A B *C* D
> The *cat* jumped *in* the sea
> The *cat* jumped *in* the sea, my friend
> How will the sad tale even end?
> E F G H my friend
> How will this sad tale even end?"

Meg had made up this song by herself. It was partly from her mother's old ABC book and partly from a song that Alva sometimes sang as she washed the dishes. Meg thought it was a good song for rinsing the laundry and munching on plums.

But Ida didn't think so at all. "Dear, dear, what a terrible song," she said. "Don't you know any nicer songs?"

"*I* think it *is* a nice song," said Meg, "but the ones you sing are nicer. Please, Ida, sing the one about the railroad to heaven."

But Ida didn't want to sing while she was doing the laundry. And it was a good thing, too, because even though Meg liked to hear the song about the heavenly railroad, it always made her cry. Just thinking about it made her very quiet, and her eyes filled with tears. It was a terribly sad song about a little girl who thought she could take the train to heaven and see her dead mother. Meg just couldn't bear to think about it on such a lovely sunny day. All Ida's songs were just as sad. The mothers all died, and the fathers neglected the children until the children all died too. Then the fathers went home and cried bitterly and were sorry for what they had done and promised never to do it again. But by then it was too late.

Meg sighed and pulled out another plum. Oh, how happy she was that her own mother was alive, right over there in their red house! Every night when Meg was saying her prayers, she added an extra one asking that she and Betsy and Mother and Father, Alva and Ida and Albert Nilsson, would all go to heaven together. Meg had an idea that it would be better never to have to go to heaven at all, because they were all so happy at home. But she didn't dare pray for that because God might be offended.

Ida was pleased when Meg cried over her songs. "There, you see how miserable the children of the poor are," she would say. "It ought to make you thankful for being so well off."

Meg knew without being told that she was well off. She had her mother and father, and Betsy, Alva, and Ida, and Albert Nilsson, and she lived at June Hill, which was the best place in the whole world. If anyone had asked her to describe it, she would have said something like this:

"It's an ordinary red house, just like other people's. The kitchen is the nicest place to be. Betsy and I play in the woodbin and we help Alva when she does the baking. But come to think of it, maybe the attic is the nicest place. Betsy and I play hide-and-seek there and sometimes we dress up as cannibals and pretend to eat people. The veranda is lots of fun too. We climb in and out through the windows and pretend we're pirates climbing up and down on a ship. There are birch trees all around the house, and I like to climb them, but Betsy can't because she is too little—only five. Sometimes I climb on the woodshed roof. The woodshed and my father's carpentry shop and the laundry are all in a red building behind our house, right next to the Nilssons' fence. When I'm sitting on the roof of the woodshed, I can look right into the Nilssons' kitchen, and that's fun. And it's fun to pretend I'm horseback riding on the mangle when Alva and Ida are in the laundry. But the river is best of all. We are allowed to sit on the landing because the water isn't deep there, but we aren't allowed to go where it's deep. In front of our house is the street. We have planted a row of lilac bushes there, so no one can see what we're doing. But we can hide behind the bushes and hear what people are saying as they walk by. Is that ever fun!"

Sometimes she really did hide behind the hedge, listening to what people said as they walked by, and sometimes they said, "What a lovely child."

Then Meg knew that Betsy was hanging on the gate, giving them her biggest smile. Meg didn't think that she herself was a lovely child, but she was happy when people said Betsy was. Everyone thought Betsy was pretty—even Ida.

"Dear, dear, she's as pretty as a picture," Ida would say.

"And good, too," Meg would say, and nibble Betsy's arm just a little, and Betsy would laugh as if Meg had tickled her.

Betsy was all softness and sweetness, but she had little sharp teeth, and she bit Meg's cheek as hard as she dared, laughing still harder and saying, "And *you* are as good as a pickle!"

There was nothing soft and sweet about Meg. She had a nice little sunburned face and laughing blue eyes and thick brown hair. She was as thin and graceful as a cat.

"She was probably never meant to be a girl," Ida sometimes said. "She should have been a boy, no doubt of that."

Meg was completely satisfied with her looks. "I look like my father, and that's fine, because it means I'll surely get married."

Betsy immediately started to worry. What if she didn't get married! Everyone said she looked like Mother. Not that she really cared much about getting married, but if Meggie did, of course Betsy had to too.

Meg gave Betsy a pat on the head. "You're much too young to think about things like that. Wait until you're as big as me and go to school."

Meg wasn't actually going to school just then, but the summer holidays would be over the next week, and Meg was looking forward to being a schoolgirl again.

"Maybe I won't get married either," she said, to console Betsy. Deep down, she couldn't really see the sense in getting married, but she had decided that if she had to it would be to Albert Nilsson, although he didn't know it yet.

Ida had just finished the laundry and Meg had finished all her plums when Betsy came down to the landing. She had been playing with Gosan on the veranda but had got tired of that and wanted to know what Meg was doing.

"Meggie," she called, "what are we going to do now?"

> "Harness a couple of cats and ride
> Over the river with the tide
> And use their tails as reins,"

Meg answered. Albert always talked in rhymes, and Meg had picked up the knack from him.

"I've already done that," said Betsy, laughing. "With Gosan, I did. And used his tail as a rein, too—on the veranda."

Meg said fiercely, "You're going to get it from me if you've been pulling Gosan's tail."

"But I didn't," said Betsy. "I didn't pull the least bit. I only held his tail. It was Gosan who tugged and pulled so hard."

Even Ida gave Betsy a severe look. "Don't you know that the angels in heaven cry so hard it rains, when children are cruel to animals?"

Betsy laughed. "But it isn't raining now."

It certainly wasn't raining. The sun was bright and warm, and the air was full of the wonderful smell of the sweet peas in the garden. The bees were humming over the grass, and the river flowed quietly and gently past June Hill. You can feel summer on your whole body, Meg thought as she kicked her feet in the warm water.

"Oh dear, oh dear, there's something not right about all this heat." Ida sighed, mopping her forehead. "It's more like rinsing the laundry in the Nile River in Africa than being up here in Sweden."

That was all Ida said, but it was enough to make an idea pop into Meg's head. Ida was right; Meg got her ideas just as quickly as a pig blinks.

"Betsy, I know what we're going to do," Meg said. "We're going to play Moses in the reeds!"

Betsy jumped up and down with delight. "Can I be Moses?"

Ida laughed. "A fine Moses you'll make!"

Ida went off to hang up her wash, and Meg and Betsy were alone on the banks of the Nile.

At night, when the lights were out in the children's room and everything was quiet, Meg told Betsy stories. Sometimes they were creepy stories about ghosts and robbers, and Betsy crawled into Meg's bed so she wouldn't be too frightened to listen. But mostly Meg told Bible stories that she had heard from Ida. So Betsy knew very well who Moses was, and that Pharaoh's daughter, an Egyptian princess, had found him lying in a basket among the reeds in the river. Moses in the reeds—that sounded like a wonderful game!

There was an empty wash boiler standing on the river bank that would be fine as an "ark of bulrushes" for Moses to be in. Betsy climbed into it at once.

"But it can't stay on land," Meg said. "That wouldn't be Moses in the reeds. Get out of the wash boiler, Betsy."

Betsy did as she was told, and Meg pushed the boiler into the water. It was heavy, but Meg was strong. There weren't a great many reeds in the river, but a big clump grew right outside the laundry, making a thick screen that hid Albert Nilsson's landing from the June Hill landing. Meg thought that was too bad, but Mother thought it a very good thing. Mother seemed to feel that the less you could see of the Nilssons the better, but Meg didn't know why. After all, people are given eyes so they can see as much as possible. But now it was very convenient to have the reeds there, because otherwise Moses wouldn't have had any reeds to lie in.

It was hard work to get the wash boiler over to the reeds. Meg and Betsy both pushed until their faces were red. But finally they managed to place it very nicely in the middle of the reed clump. Betsy climbed in and settled herself. But immediately a worried look came over her face.

"You know what," she said, "my pants are getting wet!"

"Don't fuss. They'll dry quickly when I've rescued you."

"Rescue me soon, then," said Betsy, and Meg promised. She was ready to start playing the Moses game right away. But when she looked down at her striped cotton dress she realized that Pharaoh's daughter couldn't wear that. It wouldn't look right.

"Wait," said Meg. "I'll be back in a few minutes. I have to talk to Mother."

But Mother had gone to the market, and Alva was in the basement. Meg had to try to find some princess clothes by herself. She looked around for something suitable and saw Mother's light blue silk robe hanging on a hook in the bedroom. Meg tried it on. It looked perfectly beautiful! Perhaps the real Pharaoh's daughter had one just like it when she went down to the river that day so long ago. She should also wear a veil over her hair. . . . Meg poked around in the linen closet until she found a gauzy white kitchen curtain.

She draped it over her head, and a shiver ran through her when she saw her reflection in the bedroom mirror. That was just the way Pharaoh's daughter must have looked.

In the meantime, Betsy had been sitting in her wash boiler, cozy but a bit wet. The reeds were swaying in the wind, the shimmering blue dragonflies darted in and out among the flower stalks, and tiny, tiny fish swam around the wash boiler. Betsy watched them over the side.

Then Meg came wading through the water with Mother's robe hoisted up under the arms. Betsy too thought she looked just the way Pharaoh's daughter should, and she laughed happily. She snuggled down in the wash boiler, and now the game began.

"Are you lying here all by yourself, little Moses?" asked Meg.

"Yes, I am," Betsy answered. "May I be your little boy?"

"Yes, you may," said Meg, "but first I have to rescue you from that boiler. Who put you there?"

"I did myself," said Betsy, but Meg looked at her reprovingly and whispered, "You're supposed to say, 'My mother did, so Pharaoh wouldn't kill me.'"

Betsy repeated this obediently.

"You're very lucky that I found you, little Moses. See what beautiful clothes I have."

"Yes, I am lucky," Betsy agreed.

"You'll have beautiful clothes too," said Meg. "I'm going to get you some new ones."

"And dry pants," Betsy added. "Meggie, do you know what? I think this thing is leaking."

"Quiet, Moses," Meg warned. "Soon the crocodiles will come, and they eat children. I'd better rescue you right away."

"Ab-so-lute-ly," said Betsy.

But it is quite difficult to rescue children from the Nile, as Meg soon found out. Betsy hung like a stone around her neck, and the robe dragged in the water and tangled around her legs.

"Quite a few crocodiles here." Meg puffed as she struggled toward the shore. "I think I'll take you to Nilssons' landing instead. It's closer."

"There is Albert," Betsy said.

Meg stopped dead. "Oh, is he? Get down, Betsy. You can walk by yourself."

But Betsy didn't want to. "I can't, because I'm Moses." And she tightened her grasp around Meg's neck. "I don't dare, because of the crokatiles," she said.

"There aren't any crocodiles here," Meg said fiercely. "We're not playing any more. Get down!"

But Betsy still refused. Then Meg got angry. Betsy's arms were wrapped tightly around her neck, but it would have been easy for Meg to free herself if she hadn't had Mother's robe to think about. Unless she held it up with both hands, it kept dragging in the water. So all she could do was make a series of small angry jumps, trying to shake Betsy off.

Albert was standing on the Nilssons' landing, laughing at them. "Don't jump into the deep hole," he said.

Meg knew there was a very deep place near the Nilssons' landing, but she was so furious that all she could think of was getting rid of Betsy. So she jumped and reared like a wild colt and didn't watch where she was going.

"I don't dare get down because of the crokatiles," Betsy was wailing. And then there was a splash. Meg and Betsy disappeared into the deep hole.

Perhaps they would have stayed there, perhaps there wouldn't have been any more little girls at June Hill, if Albert hadn't happened to be standing there.

He calmly picked up a boat-hook from the landing and pushed it out toward the deep hole, and immediately got a bite. When he pulled it in again, there were two wet little girls hanging on for dear life. They scrambled up onto the landing, Betsy howling like a banshee.

"Shut up, Betsy," Meg scolded. "If they hear you, we'll never be allowed to play down by the river any more."

But Betsy had no intention of stopping her howling so soon; she had hardly even begun. "Why did you have to jump into the deep hole with me?" she bawled, glaring furiously at Meg. "I'm going to tell Mother."

"You certainly are not," said Albert.

"Tattletale, tattletale!" said Meg. But suddenly she remembered that the wet, clinging garment she was wearing

was her mother's best robe. That would tattle, even if Betsy didn't.

"Come and I'll give each of you a pretzel," said Albert.

What made Albert seem so marvelous to Meg wasn't just that he was fifteen and could pull people out of the river with a boat-hook, but that he made pretzels and sold them at the market. His father was really supposed to make them and his mother to sell them, but Albert was the one who did everything. Meg felt so sorry for Albert. He wanted to be a sailor and work on a ship in real storms. He didn't want to make pretzels at all, but he had to, because his father didn't want to either. When Ida sang her sad songs about poor children whose fathers didn't take care of them, Meg always thought of Mr. Nilsson. It was true that Mr. Nilsson went on sprees only on Saturdays, but Albert had to make pretzels all week long, instead of being out on the stormy sea. Poor Albert!

If you have just been at the bottom of a river, a pretzel is very comforting. Betsy quieted down and began to munch on her pretzel, but she examined her wet dress in disgust.

"Meg, you said I would get dry when you rescued me— but just look at me!"

When Mother came home a little while later, she found her two girls in the kitchen with Alva, completely dry. They had put Sasso into the woodbin and were playing that he was a circus lion. Meg was showing him off to Alva and Betsy.

They pretended to pay two cents to see the circus lion, but they didn't have real money so they used buttons.

"Because, after all, he isn't a real lion," said Betsy, "so buttons are good enough."

On the clothesline between the apple trees, two little dresses, some underthings, and a blue silk robe were hanging with Ida's pillowcases and towels.

Mother kissed Meg and Betsy and began to unpack her market basket. "We're going to have vegetable soup for dinner," she said to Alva as she put carrots, cauliflower, and onions on the table. "And we'll have pancakes for dessert."

Then she turned to Meg and Betsy. "What have you been doing all morning?"

You could have heard a pin drop in the kitchen. Betsy gave Meg a frightened look, and Meg stared down at her foot as if she had never seen it before.

"Well, what have you been doing?" Mother asked again.

"Washing and rinsing our clothes," Meg said reluctantly. "And your bathrobe, too—that was all right, wasn't it?"

"Margaret!" said Mother.

On the clothesline the wash was flapping gently in the summer breeze, and from the Nilssons' came the sound of gay music.

> "Oh! to be rocking on the deep blue sea,
>   Free as a bird in the air"

Albert was singing as he made pretzels.

CHAPTER II

Richard

Meg had started school and was having a fine time. It made her feel so grown-up to have a reading book with a green paper cover with a label saying "Margaret Peterson, Fourth Grade"—Margaret, not Meg, because of course a schoolgirl can't be called by a baby name. It was lovely to have a little slate and a sponge tied to it with a string, and a bottle filled with water to wet the slate when it needed cleaning. And it was fun to have a slate pencil, and a pencil box to put it in, and a canvas schoolbag to put the pencil box in. But the best thing of all was the little wooden hen her father gave her, which laid pennies, one after another, when Meg was a good girl and did her homework well.

School was wonderful and on the very first day Meg had said with a sigh, "Oh dear, it's awful to think of Christmas vacation coming."

It was almost four months until Christmas, but still . . .

Meg showed the reading book, the slate, and the pencil box to Betsy, Mother, Father, Ida, Alva, and Albert Nilsson. She let Betsy thumb through the book and write a tiny bit on the slate, all the while giving a lot of advice. Every morning, when Meg left for school, Betsy stood on the veranda, wishing that she too could walk off with a beautiful schoolbag on her back. It seemed such an endless time before Meg came home, and when she finally did, she had homework to do.

She practiced her reading in the children's room, but so loudly that you could hear her all over the house.

Betsy didn't understand why anyone had to read the same thing over and over again the way Meg did, but then, she wasn't a schoolgirl.

Every day at the dinner table Father asked, "Well, Meg, how are you doing in school?"

"Fine," Meg would answer. "I'm the best one in my class."

One day Mother asked, "Who says that? You or the teacher?"

"We both think so," said Meg.

Father and Mother exchanged pleased looks. There, you see! They'd been worrying for nothing. School could make something out of even a little wildcat like Meg.

But as the days went by, Meg didn't do her homework quite so eagerly. Mother often had to remind her to do her arithmetic, and the reading was no longer heard from the children's room. There was just the usual noise of Meg and Betsy climbing on the furniture and overturning the chairs. One day there was another sound. Meg was singing.

"Put your arms around me, Adolfina,
Put your arms around me. . . ."

Mother didn't like that. "Oh, Meg, what a silly song! Who taught you that?"

Mother didn't know about the gramophone in the Nilssons' house, a strange-looking thing with a big horn. Mr. Nilsson played "Come, Adolfina" every day and danced with Mrs. Nilsson. The gramophone made a great rasping and hissing noise, but you could still hear the tune coming out of the horn.

Mother didn't seem to like the Nilssons, and she objected to Meg's visiting them, for some reason.

"Well, Meg," said Mother again, "who taught you that silly song?"

Meg began to blush. "Richard," she said. She didn't want to confess that she had heard it at the Nilssons'.

"Who is Richard?" asked Betsy.

"Richard—he is in my class," Meg said hastily.

"Oh," said Mother. "I don't think you ought to associate with that boy."

A day or two later the wooden hen laid a penny for Meg, even though she really hadn't been working as hard as she might have. For a penny she could get two pieces of butterscotch in the little candy store near the school. She promised to give Betsy one, and Betsy looked forward to it all day. When Meg finally came home, Betsy was waiting for her in the hall.

"Poor Betsy," said Meg. "Richard ate your butterscotch."

Betsy was very sad and disappointed. "Richard should have a good spanking," she said.

Richard certainly should have been spanked; because that wasn't the last time he played a mean trick.

One day Meg came home with only one of her galoshes. The other one had vanished. They were beautiful galoshes, black and shiny, with red linings.

"Where is your other galosh?" Mother asked.

"Richard threw it in the canal."

"That Richard should have a good spanking," said Betsy.

Mother was terribly annoyed with Richard. "How unfortunate to have a boy like that in your class! I think I'll have to go and have a talk with your teacher."

But Mother was so busy that she didn't get around to seeing the teacher, and Richard went on playing pranks. There was a new one almost every day.

Meg came home with a splotch of ink on her new dress —Richard, of course! One day her slate was cracked right across. Richard had thrown it against the wall because he wanted to see if it was strong. It wasn't, not that strong.

In one of Meg's books there was a picture of a queen who had lived in Sweden a long time ago. All of a sudden, one day the queen had a beard and mustache.

"But Margaret, why have you scribbled in your book?" asked Mother severely.

"I didn't. It was Richard," Meg said.

"That Richard should have a good spanking," said Betsy.

Almost every day at the dinner table Meg told stories about Richard and his terrible pranks. The teacher had a dreadful time with him. He was always making a racket in class and having to stand in the corner.

Once Meg said, "You know what he did today? He ate my eraser."

"He ate your eraser!" exclaimed Mother in a horrified voice.

"There must be something wrong with that boy," said Father.

"That Richard should have a good spanking," said Betsy.

One day Meg came home with a new hair-do. Richard had been up to tricks again. On the way home from school he had borrowed Meg's sewing scissors and cut bangs on her— and what bangs!

That was the end of Mother's patience. Such mischief couldn't be allowed to go on for another day.

"Tomorrow I'm going to school to talk to your teacher," she said firmly.

"That Richard should have—" began Betsy.

"Be quiet," Meg cried angrily. "Richard can't get a spanking, because he left school today."

"He left school?" Mother was astonished.

"Yes, he—didn't want to go to school any longer," Meg explained.

"Didn't want to!" said Mother. "What nonsense! He's probably going to another school."

"Yes, maybe he's going to another school to eat erasers," said Betsy, pleased.

Two days later Aunt Lotte had a birthday. She lived in a little yellow house right next to the school, and Mother took Meg and Betsy to wish her a happy day.

Right outside Aunt Lotte's house, whom should they meet but Meg's teacher. Meg didn't want to talk to the teacher at all, but Mother did. Meg tugged at Mother's skirt, but Mother paid no attention.

"How is Margaret doing at school?" she asked. There was really no reason to ask, because Meg herself had said that everything was fine. But Mother wanted to hear the teacher say that Meg was best in her class.

Strangely enough, the teacher didn't say that at all.

"Things will probably improve when Margaret gets a little more used to being in fourth grade," she said. "Some children have a hard time with the work at first."

Mother looked puzzled. "Do you really think that Margaret is one of those children?" What, then, could she possibly think of Richard?

"That Richard!" said Mother. "Thank goodness he has left. It must be a relief to get rid of such a troublesome child."

It was the teacher's turn to look puzzled. "Richard? We haven't had a boy named Richard."

"But—" Mother began. Then she stopped and looked severely at Meg.

"That Richard should have a good spanking," said Betsy.

Meg blushed crimson red and stared at her shoes. A spanking, Betsy said. Somebody was going to get one, but who? Meg was already missing Richard terribly.

CHAPTER III

Meg and Betsy Have a Picnic at Home

Meg never talked about Richard again. This made Betsy sad; she couldn't understand why there didn't seem to be a Richard any more. She especially missed him at the dinner table, and sometimes she would say, "I wonder what Richard is doing in his new school."

Then Meg would scowl furiously at her. Mother would pretend she hadn't heard anything, but Father would laugh and pull Meg's hair.

One day he said, "Well, Meg, you certainly spun some fine yarns, didn't you? Now suppose you tell us about school—without Richard."

Meg began by telling about the teacher's watch, such a pretty one on a long chain, and about the boys fighting in the schoolyard every day, and about what fun it was to sit in the corridor and eat sandwiches during the lunch hour.

Betsy wanted to know everything about school. "What do the children have in their sandwiches?" she asked.

"Sausage and cheese," said Meg.

Betsy sighed. How lucky some children were! They could sit in the corridor eating sandwiches with sausage and cheese, and have pencil boxes, slates, schoolbags. Betsy thought it was unfair that she couldn't go to school too.

Father went on asking questions. The next day at the dinner table he said again, "Well, how was school today?"

Meg stopped to think. Now that Richard wasn't there any more, there wasn't very much to tell. But she could always think of something.

"There's a girl called Mia in my class and she has funny little things that crawl in her hair," Meg began. "I wish I had some too."

Mother gasped. "No, thank you!"

Betsy was just about to take a mouthful of mashed potatoes, but instead she put down her fork and said triumphantly, "In my school *all* the children have funny little things in their hair."

"Don't be silly," Meg snapped. "You don't even go to school."

"I do so," Betsy insisted stubbornly.

Father laughed. "Meg isn't the only one who can tell good stories," he said. "So you have a school too, Betsy. I suppose that's the one Richard has moved to."

Betsy's face brightened. What a wonderful idea! Dresses and shoes weren't the only things she could inherit from Meg. She could inherit Richard too, and have him in her school. Betsy nodded and smiled broadly.

"Yes, Richard is in my school now, and he has so many funny little things in his hair."

"Oh, you're so silly, Betsy," said Meg crossly.

The weeks went by, and one day in late October, Meg came rushing home from school, all excited, her eyes sparkling.

"Is Mother home?" she cried as she came flying in at the door. From that moment on she didn't stop talking.

"Mother, we're going on a picnic, on Wednesday—the whole school. We're taking a train and then we're going to walk a long way and then we're going to climb to the top of a mountain and sit and eat sandwiches and look at the view. Oh, I'm so happy!"

She couldn't sit still but skipped joyfully around the room. She threw her arms around her mother, and her whole face was radiant. But Betsy's face was dark as a thundercloud. At first she greeted the news with silence, but then she said emphatically, "My school is having a picnic too, and we're taking a train and climbing a much higher mountain."

"Hoho, that's a good one!" jeered Meg.

"You're just horrid," cried Betsy and buried her head in Mother's lap, sobbing as if her heart were breaking. "I w-w-want to have a picnic too and sit on a mountain and eat sandwiches."

Then Meg felt like comforting Betsy. "We can have a picnic, the two of us," she said kindly.

Betsy cried a little longer, just to be on the safe side; then she looked up, her eyes still full of tears. "And sit on a mountain?" she asked.

"Maybe," said Meg. "If we can find one."

"That was nice of you, Meg," Mother said. "You two can have a picnic all by yourselves. That will be fun, won't it, Betsy? And you can go today, because Father and I are going to lunch at the Berglunds'.

"We'll pack a picnic basket, and you can take it to some nice place," she added, stroking Betsy's cheek.

"To a nice *mountain*," Betsy corrected her.

Mother got out the red picnic basket from the closet and filled it with good things—tiny meat balls, sausages, a couple of hard-boiled eggs, two pieces of apple cake, a bottle of milk, and two cinnamon buns.

"You and Father won't get this many good things to eat at the Berglunds'," said Meg.

Mother was in a hurry, but while she was putting on her hat and coat she cautioned Meg. "Don't go too far away, and be sure to tell Alva where you're going."

Just as she was leaving she called to Alva, "Please keep an eye on the children while I'm gone."

"Yes, ma'am, I certainly will," Alva answered as the front door closed.

Meg and Betsy carried the red basket between them. This was going to be a real picnic.

"Where can we find a mountain?" Betsy wanted to know.

Meg stood for a moment on the veranda steps, thinking. There was no mountain nearby, and Mother had said they mustn't go very far away. But, as Ida said, Meg got her ideas "as fast as a pig can blink," and she didn't have to think very long. Suddenly she remembered a story Mother had read to them a long time ago, about some children who were going on a picnic, just like Meg and Betsy, and they had a basketful of pancakes with them.

But instead of going into the woods, they climbed up on the roof of the pigsty, and all the pancakes fell down to the pigs. That had been a funny story.

"Betsy," Meg said, "we don't have a mountain, but we could climb up on the woodshed."

Betsy jumped up and down with delight. "Just like those children!" she said. "But we have no pancakes."

"And no pigs," Meg added, "so it won't make any difference if we should happen to drop the basket."

"Do you think Mother will let us?" Betsy asked.

Meg thought again for a moment. "Mother said that we should go to some nice place not too far away. The woodshed is a nice place, and from there we'll have a view just like the one I'll have on Wednesday."

Just then Alva came running out of the house. "You have to tell me where you're going."

"Not far," Meg said. "We're going to stay home."

Betsy giggled. "Not far at all. We're going to—"

"Be quiet," said Meg. "I told you, we're staying home."

Alva was satisfied and went back to finish her ironing in peace.

There was a ladder leaning against the gable end of the woodshed. Meg had used it many times to climb up on the roof. Sometimes she even walked—carefully, like someone on a tightrope—all the way over to where the branches of the Nilssons' tree hung over the laundry roof. Meg liked those little August pears.

Betsy sometimes climbed on the ladder too, but only on the lowest rungs. Now she was going to go all the way up to the roof, and it seemed both wonderful and a little alarming. But that is probably the way all picnics are, she thought.

Meg started climbing first. Although she was carrying the basket, she went up quite quickly and easily. Betsy climbed slowly behind her, and the higher up she got, the slower she went. At last the tip of her nose was above the ridge of the roof, and she could see Meg sitting there, starting to unpack all the goodies. But Betsy no longer felt that the roof was a very nice place. She was suddenly convinced that a real mountain would be much better.

"Meg, you know what?" she said in a small voice. "I don't want to climb up on this roof."

"Now don't start fussing, or there won't be any picnic," said Meg. "Come on, I'll help you."

Betsy was so frightened that she was trembling, but Meg pulled and tugged and finally managed to drag her up on the roof. Betsy moaned the whole time. "You're crazy, Meg, you're absolutely crazy."

When they were finally settled astride the ridge, with the basket between them, Betsy began to feel more at ease. "I can look right into the Nilssons' kitchen," she said.

Meg looked pleased. "Didn't I tell you we'd have a view? We can see what the Nilssons are doing. I've often been up here."

They sat there for a long time, peering through the Nilssons' kitchen window. There was Albert, baking, as usual. Mrs. Nilsson wasn't around, but Mr. Nilsson was lying on the sofa, sleeping. "What a lazy man!" Meg said.

Albert looked up and saw them and stopped his work. He moved over to the window and began to make such funny faces that they laughed until they almost fell off the roof. Meg couldn't understand how anyone could twist up his face the way Albert could. When he wasn't making faces, Meg thought he was very good looking. His hair was very blond, his eyes bright blue, and he had a nice wide mouth. But when he made all those queer faces he looked just like a troll—not handsome at all, but so funny you almost fell off the roof just looking at him.

After a while he came outside. "Hi," he said, looking up at Meg and Betsy. "How are you up there?"

"Oh, we're just fine," said Meg. Nothing could be more fun than sitting on the woodshed roof and talking to Albert.

"We're having a picnic," Betsy explained.

"So I see," said Albert. "What do you have in the basket?"

"Meat balls, sausages, and all sorts of good things," said Meg.

"Quite a lot of good things," Betsy added.

Albert was leaning on the fence that separated June Hill from Peaceful Villa—that was the name of the Nilssons' place. He was quiet and seemed to be thinking about something.

At last he said, "I bet you can't throw a meat ball into my mouth. Do you want to try?"

Meg and Betsy thought this was a splendid idea. No one could invent as many clever things as Albert. "Ha, you'll see," said Meg and quickly picked up a meat ball, which she aimed carefully at his open mouth. But the meat ball hit Albert right on the forehead and bounced off into a bed of yellow leaves. Quick as a wink Albert picked it up and stuffed it into his mouth.

"What did I tell you? You can't aim. Now you've proved it."

"We'll see this time," said Meg and picked up another

meat ball. That one whizzed right past Albert's ear and fell on the ground.

Albert picked it up, and it disappeared into his mouth. "There, you've proved it again. You just can't aim, Meg."

"Now I'm going to try," said Betsy. "I want to throw meat balls too." She tossed one without aiming at all, and it didn't even reach the fence.

"Bad shots, both of you," said Albert. He thrust a floury hand between the pickets of the fence and grabbed the meat ball.

Meg and Betsy tried several times more, but finally Meg said, "Now we couldn't aim if we wanted to, because all the meat balls are gone."

"It might be easier with the sausages," Albert suggested. "They're easier to handle. Let's try it."

Meg and Betsy were only too glad to try with the sausages. Once Meg hit Albert right between the eyes, but that was the best she could do.

"Now there are only two sausages left," Meg said, "and we're going to eat them ourselves."

"Well, don't think I have time to stand here all day just being a target for you to practice on!" said Albert. "So long, kids. Now you'll have to get yourselves another target." He disappeared into the kitchen.

"Let's have the picnic now," said Betsy, which meant that she wanted to start eating.

They ate the last two sausages, the eggs, the apple cake,

and the cinnamon buns. Everything tasted good, and they had more than enough to eat even though they had tossed away the meat balls and almost all the sausages. As they were drinking their milk, Betsy's glass overturned, and a small white rivulet ran down the tiles toward the gutter.

"Just think how surprised the sparrows will be when they find milk in the gutter," Meg said.

"Yes, and happy, too," said Betsy. "What are we going to do now, Meggie?"

"We have to look at the view a little longer, because that's the reason for going on picnics," Meg explained.

"Is it?" asked Betsy doubtfully.

"Yes, that's what the teacher says, and that's what we're going to do on Wednesday. But the boys say they don't care about the view. They just want to have fun."

But Meg and Betsy were not like the boys. They stared at the view as hard as they could, and not only into the Nilssons' kitchen. They turned their heads in every direction, just as you're supposed to do on a picnic. They could see the river all the way to the bend, the willow trees leaning out over the water, and the houses and gardens along the banks. The yellow and red autumn leaves were beautiful, and the sky was blue and clear. They leaned backward and gazed at the sky, so as not to miss seeing every possible view. A bird was flying high over their heads.

"What a view he must have!" exclaimed Meg. "I wish I could fly."

"People can't fly," said Betsy.

"Yes, in airplanes they can," Meg corrected her. "Albert has told me all about airplanes." Meg would have given anything to see an airplane, although Ida had told her it was a sin to fly. "If God wanted people to fly, he would have made birds of them," said Ida.

Betsy said she thought airplanes were very strange. "But they aren't the only ones that can fly. Peter Pan can fly too, you know."

"Oh, you're silly, Betsy," said Meg. But then the wheels started going round in her mind. Albert had once told her that during the war people jumped down from airplanes with big umbrellas. Of course Meg understood that it wasn't possible to fly all over the place, but it seemed to work all right if you just wanted to come down to earth from an airplane, or some other high place. Meg pondered this. The woodshed was a high place. . . .

"I think I'll try," said Meg.

"Try what?" Betsy asked.

"To fly with an umbrella," was Meg's solemn answer.

When Betsy heard what Meg was planning to do, she laughed so hard that she cried.

"You're crazy, Meggie," she said. "Are we going to pretend that you're Peter Pan?"

"No, we're *not* going to pretend that I'm Peter Pan. Don't be silly. Don't you see? I'm going to make believe that I'm jumping out of an airplane."

"You are crazy, Meggie," said Betsy again.

Somehow Meg would have to sneak Father's big umbrella out of the stand in the hall without Alva's seeing her, because she wasn't at all sure that Alva would understand about flying with an umbrella. Perhaps she'd never heard how things are done in wars, and she might start trouble.

Betsy stopped laughing when she realized that she was going to be left alone on the roof, but Meg consoled her. "You can watch the Nilssons while I'm away. Just sit still and don't move, and you won't fall down." With this Meg disappeared down the ladder.

She wandered over casually to take a look into the kitchen. Alva was standing there, ironing and perspiring. She had to keep the fire going in order to keep the irons hot, and the kitchen was like an oven, even with the windows open.

"I'm glad you're here, so I don't have to go out to keep an eye on you. How is the picnic going?"

"Just fine," said Meg.

"Where is Betsy?" Alva wanted to know.

"She is at the—picnic place," said Meg and slipped into the hall before Alva had a chance to ask any more questions. There was Father's umbrella in the umbrella stand. Meg grabbed it as Alva opened the door.

"Is Sasso with you?" she asked.

"No," said Meg, trying to hide the umbrella behind her back.

"Then he's run away, as usual," said Alva. "What are you doing with that umbrella?"

"I thought—in case it should rain . . ."

"Rain—today! That's the silliest thing I've ever heard. Put that umbrella back!"

Meg was annoyed. She didn't have time to stand here discussing the weather when she was about to fly for the first time in her life.

"You should always have an umbrella on a picnic," she said. "Suppose it *should* rain. Then we'd really be in a fix."

Alva laughed. "The weather wouldn't change any faster than you could run for shelter on the veranda. But take the umbrella, if you insist. Be sure to bring it back, though, or your father will be cross."

"Yes, yes, yes," said Meg impatiently and dashed out the veranda door.

Everything was so quiet you wouldn't have thought there was a living creature at June Hill. A most remarkable flight was about to take place, and there wasn't a soul to watch— no one, that is, but Betsy. Alva's kitchen window looked in the other direction, Albert had disappeared into Peaceful Villa, Mr. Nilsson was still sound asleep on the sofa.

So only Betsy was there to see Meg's flight. Only Betsy saw how Meg stood on the edge of the roof and opened the big black umbrella. Only Betsy saw how she lifted it high over her head and got ready to jump.

"You're crazy," said Betsy. "You're ab-so-lute-ly crazy."

"Silly, it isn't dangerous," Meg retorted—though the ground looked very far away. But after all, if people could jump from airplanes a couple of thousand feet up in the air, then it certainly should be possible to do it from the wood-shed roof.

Meg stood poised for a moment, holding the umbrella over her head, and made noises like an airplane. Albert had never even seen or heard an airplane, but he knew what they sounded like and had taught Meg. Albert seemed to know everything.

"Puttputtputt," stuttered Meg.

"Oh, dear!" wailed Betsy.

Then Meg took off. She walked right out into the air. Then there was a thud.

"That went quicker than lightning," Betsy cried. She wriggled on her stomach to the edge of the roof and peered down. Meg was lying absolutely still, with her face toward the ground, and didn't answer. Beside her was the umbrella, its handle broken in two.

"What's the matter with you?" cried Betsy. "Are you dead?"

Meg still didn't answer.

"Meggie, tell me if you're dead," screamed Betsy frantically. There was no sound from Meg. Then Betsy began to scream in earnest. "Mother! Mother!"

She felt as if she were all alone in the world, and she couldn't even get down from the roof.

In the midst of her shouting, Mr. Nilsson poked his head out of the window. "What are you doing up there, and why are you making such a racket?"

"Meggie is dead," cried Betsy. "Meggie is dead."

Mr. Nilsson quickly climbed out of the window and jumped over the fence. He knelt on the grass beside Meg and turned her face toward him. She was very pale, and there was blood on her forehead.

Now Alva came running. She stopped and moaned at the sight of Meg. "What in heaven's name has happened?"

Mr. Nilsson sadly shook his head. "It's all over," he said in a hushed voice. "There is no more little Meg at June Hill."

CHAPTER IV

A Sad Happy Day

Meg was lying in bed with a bandage around her head. She wasn't allowed to move.

"Only when you feel sick," said Betsy. "Then you can move a little."

Meg wasn't dead, and Betsy was happy about that. She just had a brain concussion, which isn't as bad as being dead. It makes you feel pretty sick, but you don't die, Dr. Berglund said.

Just the same, all of June Hill had been in an uproar when Meg had tried to fly and then wouldn't wake up for a long time. Mother had cried, and Father had cried—but not as much as Mother—and Alva had cried harder than Mother and Father put together.

"It's all my fault," Alva groaned. "But how could I guess that she was taking the umbrella to fly with?"

Now Meg lay in bed and couldn't remember at all what it felt like to fly, which annoyed her very much because that meant that it was all for nothing. On top of everything, she had this miserable brain concussion. She had to stay in bed at least four days, Dr. Berglund said.

Meg had let out a shriek when Mother told her. "Four days—that's impossible! The school picnic is on Wednesday and I'm—"

"You certainly are not," said Mother. "You've had enough picnicking."

Betsy nodded in agreement. "You've had enough picnics! Now you have to lie in bed and be sick."

At that Meg started a real earthquake. That was what Father called it when she got furious and desperate as only Meg could. The tears streamed down her face, and she screamed so loud she could be heard all over the house.

"I want to go on the picnic! I'm going on the picnic! Oh, I wish I were dead."

Betsy looked at her curiously and tried to console her. "In my school *all* the children have brain concussions and can't go on any picnics at all."

Mother also tried to console Meg. "If you cry that way, your headache will become worse."

"I don't care." Meg went on howling. "I wish I were dead!"

Mother looked sad and went out of the room. Ida was down in the kitchen, helping Alva to can applesauce, and when she heard the wild shouts she came up to the children's room and looked severely at Meg.

"Margaret, Margaret, now you're being sinful. Think of what the Bible says, and don't lie here wishing yourself dead."

But Meg didn't want to think about anything but the picnic, and she screamed at Ida. "Leave me alone!"

Ida shook her head and looked worried. "So that's the way it is," she said. "I see that Sebastian Loki is back in the house!"

Ida couldn't think of anything worse than Sebastian Loki. He came to the house when Meg and Betsy were not as good as Ida thought they ought to be. The person lying in bed screaming wasn't Meg at all. It was really Sebastian Loki, and the real Meg, the good little girl, was sitting up in the chimney until Sebastian Loki decided it was time to leave.

"What bad luck that he happened to come today," said Ida.

"That's all right," said Betsy, "because now *he* can have the headache and feel sick, and Meg can sit in the chimney and have a lot of fun."

Meg just glared at Ida and Betsy. The business about Sebastian Loki was all right for Betsy, but Meg was too big for such childish nonsense.

"Calm down," said Ida. "Just be happy you're alive. You weren't far from flying yourself to death."

But Meg couldn't be happy. She pulled the covers over her head and cried.

Every morning for the next few days she woke up hoping for a miracle—such as Mother coming into her room and saying, "What's a little brain concussion, anyway? Besides, picnics are the best cure for brain concussions. Don't you think you'll be well enough to go along on Wednesday, after all?"

But Mother didn't say anything of the kind. She only stroked Meg's cheek and smiled encouragingly. "Don't be sad," she said. "We'll think of something else that will be fun."

Something else that's fun! As if there could be anything in the whole wide world that was fun except that picnic!

On Tuesday night Meg prayed for help. She lay with the covers pulled over her head and whispered so that Betsy wouldn't hear her, "Please, God, help me! Because I would so much like to go. Make Doctor Berglund call Mother and tell her I'm fine—because I am! But do it right away if we're going to manage everything on time. I have to have sandwiches and chocolate, and Alva has to iron my new sailor dress. So please tell Doctor Berglund to call immediately. Please, dear God, because I would so much like to go. Amen."

Then Meg lay there, listening intently for the telephone to ring. But no telephone rang. All she heard was Betsy, who kept nagging from her bed. "Tell me stories about ghosts and cops and robbers."

But Meg didn't want to tell stories. She lay for a long

time listening for the telephone that never rang. Then she cried a little under the covers before she fell asleep.

On Wednesday morning she woke up early. The sun was shining in a blue, blue sky. What a wonderful day for all the lucky schoolchildren who didn't have a brain concussion! She peered at the clock—almost eight, just the time the train would be leaving. All her classmates would be gathered at the station, and she could just see them laughing and talking and rushing into the train, squabbling about the window seats, and having a good time while they waited for the train to pull out.

Meg stared miserably at the cuckoo clock hanging on the wall above her bed. She watched the hands move as it ticked closer and closer toward eight. Then the cuckoo popped out and called, "Cuckoo," eight times. Meg burst into tears because she knew the train had left. Poor, poor Meg, having to stay in bed and never having any fun!

Betsy woke up in fine spirits. She didn't realize what a sad day it was and sang the "ABCD" song just the way Meg had taught her.

Meg snapped at her. "Be quiet, you horrid little brat. Be quiet, I tell you! *Shut up!*"

"Oh, so Sebastian Loki is back," said Betsy calmly, sounding just like Ida.

Just then the door opened and Mother came in, carrying a tray beautifully arranged with two great big blue cups of hot chocolate on it, and waffles.

Betsy opened her eyes wide. "Is it my birthday?" she asked.

"No," said Mother, "but sometimes it's nice to celebrate without a birthday. Sit up, Meggie, and have some hot chocolate and waffles."

Meg slowly crawled out from under the bedclothes. Her eyes were wet. Mother kissed her and served her chocolate and waffles. Without a word Meg began to eat. She sat there, quietly stuffing herself with one waffle after another. There were still tears on her eyelashes, and this was a very sad day, but just the same the waffles and hot chocolate were delicious.

Betsy heartily agreed. "It tastes just like a regular birthday."

"Of course it does," said Mother as she left the room. Betsy's breakfast had disappeared rapidly, and she licked the last traces of sugar and butter from her fingers before she climbed purposefully out of bed. Just as she finished dressing, the doorbell rang.

"It's the mailman," she said. "Meggie, do you want me to go down and see if there is anything for us?"

Betsy and Meg didn't often get any mail, but to be on the safe side they looked in the mailbox every morning. Now Meg just shrugged her shoulders. This was a sad day, so why should there be any mail? Betsy ran down anyway. Meg was left alone, and her thoughts went back to the picnic. She looked at the clock. The train ride must be over by now, and they'd probably be walking along the road, singing. She could see them clearly as they went marching along, two by two. Now they would have reached the mountain where they were going to have the picnic—and here was Meg, lying in bed and never having any fun.

Then Betsy came running up the stairs, completely out of breath. "Meggie, guess what?" she cried. "You have three cards and a package!"

"I *have?*" Meg sat up eagerly in bed.

Meg and Betsy collected postcards, and each of them had an album almost full. On birthdays and holidays they received the most wonderful cards. Sometimes there were flowers on them, sometimes dear little kittens or puppies, and sometimes handsome men with beards, and ladies in beautiful dresses. Some of the cards were shiny, and those were the most beautiful of all. Now Meg had got three of these shiny cards all at once, although there was no birthday or holiday to celebrate—just a brain concussion. Meg was thrilled with her cards. Oh, how beautiful they were! On the first one there was a white dove holding a red rose in its beak, on the second a pink angel soaring in a dark blue sky full of shiny gold stars, and on the third a little boy dressed in velvet with a bouquet of yellow roses. Meg looked at them all and sighed with bliss.

"Look and see who sent them," Betsy reminded her, and Meg quickly turned the cards over.

"From a friend," it said in printed letters on all three of them.

"What do you think that means?" asked Meg.

Their cards usually came from Grandmother or the cousins, not from "a friend." To receive cards from an unknown friend was something very new and strange.

"Perhaps they're from Albert," Betsy suggested.

"Sending me *three* cards?" said Meg. "He's not crazy, I hope." She was so happy about the cards that she had almost forgotten about the package. But now she pounced on it and began to unwrap it.

There was a box inside, and inside the box a lot of pink tissue paper. Meg and Betsy looked at each other, quivering with excitement. Almost anything could be inside that pink paper, and it was a delightful feeling not to know what it was. Meg bent down and sniffed it.

"What do you suppose it could be?"

Betsy sniffed at the paper. "I don't know."

"Do you think I ought to look?" asked Meg.

"Ab-so-lute-ly," said Betsy.

The tissue paper rustled under Meg's eager fingers, while Betsy held her breath.

Under the top layer there was a letter. "To Meggie from Grandmother," it said on the envelope. But that wasn't all! Underneath there was a tiny baby doll, and a tiny little bathtub for the baby to bathe in, and a tiny little bottle to feed her with, and a tiny piece of soap to wash her with. And then there was a tiny little bag of beads to make necklaces with, and two little green boxes with pretty pictures on the covers, each with a pink candy and a ring inside. Betsy's eyes opened wide as she looked at everything. She was very quiet for a minute, and then she said solemnly, "I wish I could have a brain concussion too."

Meg took one of the little boxes in each hand. "Which one would you like?" she asked. "Would you rather have a ring with a red stone or a ring with a blue stone?"

"A green one," said Betsy.

"Silly, there isn't any green one," said Meg.

"Then I'll take a blue one," Betsy said. "Oh, that's awfully nice of you, Meggie."

Meg herself thought it was awfully nice of her, and it felt good not to be sad any longer, and not to have to think about the picnic.

"Mountains are all right," she said, "but I still think we had a better view from the woodshed."

"Ab-so-lute-ly," said Betsy, "because we could look into the Nilssons' kitchen."

Meg and Betsy put their rings on. They stretched out their fingers and felt like elegant ladies.

"My stone looks like a drop of blood," said Meg. "What does yours look like?"

"Mine looks like blue," said Betsy, and that, of course, was true.

For a long time they compared rings. They put their hands next to each other and discussed which was the prettier. It ended with Meg thinking that red stones are prettier because they look like drops of blood, and Betsy thinking that blue stones are prettier because they're blue.

Meg suddenly remembered that she hadn't read Grandmother's letter, and tore open the envelope. Grandmother had printed the letter, because Meg couldn't read handwriting very well yet.

Betsy couldn't understand how Meg figured out what Grandmother said just by looking at some squiggles in a letter. "Can you really read that?" she asked.

Of course Meg could read it! When she had spelled her way through the letter, she knew exactly what Grandmother wanted. She wanted Meg to give up flying completely, and she wanted Meg to give Betsy one of the little boxes and half of the beads in the bead bag.

"Don't you think I'm kind, Betsy? I gave you the box *before* I read the letter," Meg said.

"Yes, you were very kind," said Betsy and grabbed the bead bag. "Give me my beads. Now I'm going to make a necklace."

But Meg pulled the bead bag out of her hand. "Leave them alone," she said. "You have to wait until I have time to divide them."

"You have time now," said Betsy.

"I just don't happen to feel like it."

She poured a glass of water from the carafe on the table beside her bed and drank in long, slow swallows until the glass was empty. Then she took the pink tissue paper and began to fold it very carefully. She folded and folded, so that anyone could see that she was too busy to count out beads. All this time she was thinking. The little box was a better present than a bag of beads. Still, it was easier to give the box to Betsy than to divide the beads with her. Meg wanted very much to keep all the beads. But she knew that if Betsy didn't get any she would go to Mother and tattle, and then Meg would have to share them with her anyway. She replaced the tissue paper in the box as neatly and carefully and deliberately as she could, and then she sighed and said, "Now I have time."

She poured the beads onto a tray and divided them into two even piles. One big yellow bead was left over, and this she gave to Betsy. "You take it," she said, for Meg was never stingy for more than a few minutes at a time.

When Meg and Betsy had made necklaces and put them on, they were even more elegant than before.

Then they played with the little baby doll. They bathed her in the little tub, washing her with the little soap, which smelled perfectly delicious. Then they made a bed for her in a cigar box and gave her a bottle.

"This is a very sad day," said Meg, "but we're having fun."

Betsy heartily agreed. "Yes, it's a sad, happy day."

But after a while she got bored and wanted to go outside. "I'm going to take Sasso for a walk," she said and was gone in a flash.

It was no fun playing alone, and soon Meg was bored and

couldn't think what to do. But then Father came home for lunch and stopped in to see her.

"How do you feel?" he asked.

"Fine," said Meg, "but I have nothing to do."

"You can read the paper," Father said and took it out of his pocket. "Here is a pad, too. Make a good drawing to give me when I come home for dinner."

Meg had learned to read so capably that even the teacher was surprised. When Father had gone, she immediately opened the newspaper, but she didn't understand much of what it said. There was a lot about war, and advertisements about pigs and cows for sale, about people who had got married or engaged, and about women's coats and dresses. There was a great deal more, but none of it interested Meg.

She read the headings. One column was called "From Long Ago." Could that possibly be any fun? She didn't know what "long ago" was, but she soon found out. It was all about what people did years and years before Meg was born. Poor things, how bored they must have been! She sighed and put the paper down. It certainly was strange that Father was so funny and gay, and yet wrote such a dull newspaper. Since he was the editor, he must decide what was going to be in it, but why couldn't he find anything amusing to write about? It probably wasn't easy to write newspapers. She decided to make a newspaper so she could find out for herself. It wouldn't be printed, of course, but she could write it on the pad, and she could cut the headlines out of Father's paper. Then everything would look almost right.

With her pad and pencil, a pair of scissors, and some paste in front of her on the tray, Meg got to work. She cut "From Long Ago" out of Father's paper and pasted it at the top of the pad. Then she had to say something underneath. She chewed thoughtfully on her pencil and then wrote:

Now I am going to tell what the children did a long time ago. They were good to their Mothers, but some were mean. Not so very good, exactly. They had flint axes, but they soon learned to shoot with guns.

But Meg soon got tired of times gone by. She cut out a news headline from Father's paper: "From the War Front." She pasted that on a new page of the pad. Again she chewed on her pencil. After thinking for a while she wrote:

The war is terrible. The soldiers lie in trenches and have cold feet. But a soldier jumped down from an airplane with an umbrella and didn't get a brain concussion.

That ended the war for Meg. She looked through Father's paper to get some new ideas. "Notices." They were probably an important part of a real newspaper.

She cut out the heading "Deceased" and pasted it on a new page. Then she gnawed on her pencil, deep in thought.

After a while she began to write, looking very pleased with herself. When she had finished, she drew a black border around what she had written.

Then she decided that she didn't want to make a newspaper any longer. It would be more fun to draw. So she made a picture for her father which showed her flying from the woodshed, and it turned out very well. She gave it to Father when he came home for dinner, and he thought it was good too.

Meg sat up at the table for dinner, dressed in a bathrobe. Maybe she wasn't strong enough to go on picnics, but she was strong enough to eat, especially dessert.

Later on, when Meg and Betsy were lying in their beds, ready to go to sleep, Mother and Father came in to say good night. Mother told them a story about Prince Hatt who lived under the ground, and Father made shadow figures on the wall. At first the light was too dim, so Father took off the lampshade. Then the shadow figures became very clear as they moved on the wall. Sometimes there was a goat with two big horns, sometimes a girl dancing—and yet they were only the shadows of Father's fingers!

It was so nice to have both Mother and Father in the room at the same time that Meg wished she could keep them there for hours and hours. But after a while Mother said, "Now you must go to sleep!"

Betsy was already asleep, but Meg lay awake for a long time, thinking about the picnic again. It was all over now, and the day after tomorrow she would go back to school, and she knew that all her classmates would be talking about what a marvelous time they had had. But not Meg. Oh, *why* couldn't she have been there?

She could see a great many stars through the crack at the top of the window shade, and they looked bigger than usual. They were almost as pretty as the stars on her card, the one with the angels. She tried to count them, but it didn't work. You get sleepy when you count stars.

Now all of June Hill was sleeping by its peaceful river, among the white birch trees. Mother was the only one in the whole house who was still awake. She tiptoed into the children's room to tuck in her girls, and found a paper lying on the floor near Meg's bed. She picked it up and read by the light of the night lamp:

Deceased. Thank goodness our nasty, mean Sebastian Loki is dead. He doesn't want to be buried.

On Friday morning Meg went to school. She dragged her feet unwillingly because she didn't want to hear about the picnic.

Twenty minutes later she came storming home again. She flew into the kitchen, almost frightening her mother to death. Mother thought something terrible must have happened. Why else would Meg come home during school hours, looking so wild?

"Mother, Mother," Meg cried, panting, "we're going to

have a picnic . . . now . . . today . . . there wasn't any on Wednesday . . . the teacher tripped on the stairs . . . oh, I'm so happy . . . she got a brain concussion too . . . I want hot chocolate in a Thermos . . . where is my dress . . . quick, Mother, quick."

When Ida came to do the Friday cleaning a little while later, she met Meg at the gate of June Hill. Meg was wearing a new dress and a sailor hat, and her face was glowing. Her knapsack bounced on her back as she pranced gaily along.

"I'm going on a picnic," she said. "I'm so happy!"

"Oh," said Ida, "wasn't it you who was lying in bed, screaming and wanting to be dead? Today everything seems to have changed."

Meg laughed. "That was Sebastian Loki who wanted to be dead, and he is dead, too. It says so in the paper."

"Which paper?" asked Ida.

"I'm not going to tell," Meg said, laughing again. Then she took off for her picnic. She was going on a train, she was going to sit on a mountaintop and eat sandwiches. Small wonder that sparks seemed to fly around her.

CHAPTER V

Meg Experiments to See
if She Is Clairvoyant

Mother didn't really like Meg to visit the Nilssons, but Meg couldn't think of a nicer place than their kitchen.

One day she heard her father say to her mother, "Let her go. I want my children to know that there are different kinds of people. Then maybe they will learn not to be too quick to judge."

Meg wasn't supposed to hear this, so she couldn't ask Father why people were not supposed to be quick to judge. Perhaps Father meant that she shouldn't be cross with Mr. Nilsson because he was lazy. Meg wasn't cross with him, because Mr. Nilsson was always nice to her and called her "Little Meggie from June Hill." He was never mean to Albert or Mrs. Nilsson, either.

"When I'm home in Peaceful Villa I want to be left in

peace," Mr. Nilsson would say and lie down on the kitchen sofa. "One can't just work and slave for wife and children. One has to rest *sometime*."

Mrs. Nilsson understood that Mr. Nilsson needed rest, but sometimes she couldn't see why he needed quite so much rest. When the garbage truck came along, for instance, Mrs. Nilsson didn't want to carry the trash can to the gate herself, and she made Mr. Nilsson do it. But he didn't like that at all.

Afterward he would lie on the sofa and not speak to Mrs. Nilsson for a long while. He would just stare up at the ceiling and say sadly to himself, "Here I am, a respectable house- and property-owner, having to carry the trash can all the way to the gate."

But when Mr. Nilsson played the phonograph and danced with Mrs. Nilsson, and the whole house was fragrant with the smell of Albert's freshly baked pretzels, then the Nilssons' kitchen was a lovely place to be. Alva, who sometimes came to take Meg home, said it was dirtier than any place she had ever seen in her whole life. But how many places had Alva really seen? Maybe the Nilssons didn't sweep so very often, and they didn't wash the dishes unless it was really necessary. But Meg thought it was clean enough just the same. Mrs. Nilsson embroidered covers for her shelves saying in letters of red yarn: "A Place for Everything and Everything in Its Place." On the longest one she had embroidered, "Sunshine outside, sunshine inside."

"One day I'm going to take them down and wash them,"

Mrs. Nilsson would say. "Then it will be easier to read the embroidery."

"You don't read it anyway." Mr. Nilsson would chuckle and take her around the waist and dance and sing:

> "Come, Adolfina, pretty Adolfina,
> Put your arms around me.
> Come, Adolfina,
> Dance a waltz with me. . . ."

"Oh, what a silly you are!" Mrs. Nilsson would say and laugh heartily.

Over at the baking table Albert would be whistling, "Come, Adolfina," as he shaped pretzels in time to the music.

But the best times of all were when Albert and Meg were alone in the kitchen. Albert knew about so many things and told Meg wonderful stories while he went on with his baking. Meg would sit on the kitchen sofa, just listening. Almost all the stories she told Betsy she had first heard from Albert. He had met only three bandits, but he had seen many ghosts. Meg had never seen a single one.

One day she asked him why this was. "It's because I'm clairvoyant," Albert replied. "You have to be; otherwise you can't see ghosts."

Clairvoyant—that was a word Meg had never heard before, but Albert explained it to her. "If you're clairvoyant it means that you have a special kind of eyes so that you can see ghosts and phantoms when ordinary people can't."

Albert said it was surprising that there could be such a difference. "I don't understand it—an ordinary human being can actually bump right into a ghost without knowing it."

"Do you think I'm an ordinary human being?" Meg asked, and added eagerly, "Perhaps I'm clairvoyant too. Maybe I've just never been in a place where there are ghosts."

Albert burst out laughing. "You, clairvoyant! You're no more clairvoyant than a pig."

For a while he worked quietly at his pretzels. Then he said, "But of course I could take you to the cemetery some dark night to test you."

Meg shuddered. "The cemetery—are there ghosts there?"

"You bet," said Albert. "I've seen ghosts in other places too, but in the cemetery they are lined up in bands like tin soldiers. You can hardly move without bumping into one."

Meg would have liked very much to know whether she was clairvoyant, but she had no desire to go in the middle of the night to a cemetery swarming with ghosts. "Isn't there any place where there aren't quite so many of them?" she asked.

Albert's light blue eyes fixed her with a stare. "Are you a coward?"

Meg looked uncomfortable and didn't answer. It would be awful to have Albert think she was a coward, but worse still to go to the cemetery in the middle of the night.

Albert looked at her thoughtfully. "Of course I could test

you someplace else," he said and tossed a pretzel onto the bake board. "Our laundry, for example, is haunted."

"Is it?" Meg was amazed. She had been in the Nilssons' laundry many times but she had never seen the tiniest ghost or phantom. Could that mean that she really was no more clairvoyant than a pig?

"I don't think it's worth the trouble," Albert said, "but we could try just the same. Tonight, maybe?"

Meg fidgeted uncomfortably. "Does it have to be at night?"

"Well, what do *you* think? Do you think the ghost helps Mother with the washing? No, midnight is the time he shows himself, not a minute before."

"Why does he hang around your laundry?" asked Meg.

Albert didn't answer for a while, and then he said, "Well, I may as well tell you the whole story. It's really a secret, and you have to promise not to say a word about it to a living soul."

Meg was so excited that she began to prickle with goose-flesh. Albert knew she never gave away secrets, so she must be the only one he would tell about the ghost in the laundry. Never had Meg heard anything more amazing.

Albert told her that the ghost was none other than his own grandfather's grandfather, who had lived a hundred years ago and was a very rich baron. Albert said he himself was practically a baron, though he kept it a secret. Meg gazed at him, her eyes big as saucers. She had never heard *anything* to equal this.

"Do you know why my grandfather's grandfather can't keep still like all the other old dead barons? Do you know why he has to roam around the laundry every night?"

Meg didn't know, but Albert could explain it. That rich old baron had buried a whole lot of money in his brewery, which Mrs. Nilsson now used as a laundry.

"It was only for the fun of it," Albert said. "He had put so much money in the banks that there wasn't room for any more, and then he thought of the brewery. After he had buried the money there he died, and that's why he keeps on hanging around here in such a state. That's why his ghost is haunting this place."

Meg could hardly breathe. "Do you mean that the money is *here?*"

"Of course," said Albert.

Meg stared at him. "Why don't you dig it up?" she asked.

"Try to dig it up yourself and you'll see how easy it is. Do you know *where* to dig?"

No, of course Meg didn't know.

"Well, then," said Albert, as if that settled the matter.

Meg was looking at him as if she had never seen him before. There he stood, matter-of-factly making pretzels, although he was really a baron and had a grandfather's grandfather who was also a baron—and a ghost into the bargain!

"What's his name—the ghost—your grandfather's grandfather, I mean?"

Albert stopped in the middle of twisting a pretzel. When

he finally answered, it was as if he were reading out of a book.

". . . and his name was Baron Albert Nilsson . . . Crow."

That sounded so elegant and so imposing that Meg got gooseflesh again.

"It's a good thing I'm not a snob," said Albert. " 'The Right Honorable Baron Albert Nilsson Crow'—that's what you should call me, actually. But it doesn't matter. You can keep on calling me Albert."

"Yes, because otherwise I couldn't talk to you," said Meg. "But I'll call you 'the Right Honorable Albert' sometimes, if you like."

But Albert said he'd rather she didn't. All he wanted was to have Meg go with him to the laundry at midnight, because, if she should be clairvoyant, she could help to push Baron Crow into a corner, and then at last it might be possible to talk to him about the money. Albert had tried several times, but his grandfather's grandfather had just disappeared through the wall with a faint hollow sigh.

Meg was beginning to wonder whether it was really so important to be clairvoyant. She certainly would have liked to see a ghost, but not if she had to chase Albert's grandfather's grandfather around the laundry in the middle of the night.

"Mother would never allow me to go out in the middle of the night," she said.

Albert felt very sorry for anyone who could be so silly.

"Dumbbell, were you going to tell your mother? Why, you'll never find out if you're clairvoyant. Believe me!"

Meg was sure he was right, for she knew Mother wanted her to sleep at night, clairvoyant or not.

Then Albert reminded her of all the times she had climbed out of her room by way of the veranda roof. That had been during the day, of course, but what you could do in the day-time you could also do at night—if you weren't afraid to, that is.

"Well, are you coming or aren't you?" Albert asked severely.

Meg didn't know what to say. "Maybe I wouldn't be able to stay awake until midnight," she faltered at last.

But Albert wasn't going to let her off so easily. He pondered for a while and then said, "I think that I might be able to trick the old man into coming a little earlier, for once. Can you guess how?"

Meg couldn't. She wasn't as clever as Albert.

"I'll put my alarm clock in the laundry and set it ahead three hours. What do you think of that? Then the old man will think it's twelve o'clock when it's really only nine."

Meg echoed his triumphant laugh, but she didn't sound very happy.

"Well, are you coming?" asked Albert more severely than before.

"Ye-e-es, I guess so," Meg said hesitantly.

"Fine," said Albert. "I can depend on you."

Meg and Betsy usually went to bed at seven o'clock, and Mother came into their room to tell them stories and sing to them for a while. Then they all sang a song together, Mother, Meg, and Betsy, and sometimes Father was there too, and they'd sing rounds like "Oh, how lovely is the evening, when the bells are sweetly ringing." Meg was always happy when she heard that beautiful melody, and the words made her happy too, although she didn't understand why.

It was peaceful and quiet to be lying in a soft bed after Mother had tucked you in, listening to the wind whispering in the birch trees outside the window.

But that night was far from peaceful and quiet. Meg shivered when she thought about what she had agreed to do, but it was a rather pleasant sort of shivering that she didn't really mind. Something in Meg always pushed her toward adventure, and she thrived on excitement. She had quite made up her mind that she would go to Mrs. Nilsson's laundry and find out whether she was clairvoyant. It was like going to the dentist; the worst part is before you get there, and afterward it's not so bad. If Albert could stand to see ghosts, so could Meg. At least, that's what she thought as long as she was lying safe in bed.

Long after Mother and Father had said good night, Meg lay waiting for Betsy to fall asleep. This was such a deep, dark secret that not even Betsy could be in on it.

Meg whispered, "Are you asleep?"

"No," answered Betsy. "Are you?"

"Oh, you're so silly," Meg said crossly. She lay quiet for a while, then tried again.

"Betsy, are you sleeping?"

"Not really," said Betsy. "Are you?"

"What a nuisance you are!" Meg was very annoyed. "Are you thinking of lying awake all night?"

"Ab-so-lute-ly," said Betsy.

But the next minute she turned over on her stomach and fell asleep.

Meg had never got dressed in the dark before. She didn't dare turn on the light because Betsy might wake up, or Mother might see the glimmer under the door. But Meg had put her clothes neatly on the chair next to her bed, so that she could get into them quickly. She had one terrible moment. She could find only one sock! She felt around desperately for the other. It wouldn't be proper to go wearing only one sock, to see Albert's grandfather's grandfather who was a baron. At last she found the sock under the chair beside her shoes. It wasn't easy to lace the shoes in the dark, but she did the best she could, and then there was only her dress left to put on, and her sweater. Now she was ready for the worst part, and Meg clenched her teeth. She had to open the door and tiptoe across the hall to the little window that opened onto the veranda roof, so quietly that Mother and Father wouldn't hear her. They were down in the living room, and when Meg opened the door she could hear them talking.

She got to the window without any mishap and managed to open it, though there was a terrible squeak as she pushed it up. Down in the living room there was a sudden silence, and Meg stopped dead, her heart pounding. What was going to happen now?

All that happened was that Mother began to play a peaceful little melody on the piano. The sound of the music died away as Meg crawled over the veranda roof, and she felt a pang of despair. She was leaving peace and warmth and safety behind, and ahead were only darkness and danger.

That dark, cold November night was gloomier than Meg could have believed possible. The wind that had sounded so gentle before now seemed to lash through the leafless trees, rattling the branches as if to frighten people.

Meg stood in the dark outside the Nilssons' kitchen window, looking in at Albert and his mother and father. She would have loved to go inside where it was light and warm, but Albert had said that she was to stand by the window and make sounds like an owl. Meg did as she was told, and the sounds were so eerie that she even frightened herself. She saw Mrs. Nilsson jump with alarm, and Albert too was startled. He got up from his chair, put his cap on, and went to the door. Watching him in the dim light, Meg thought he didn't look very elegant for a baron. His pants were patched at the knees, and his sweater hung like a sack on his thin frame. Meg had an idea that barons were usually fatter and better groomed, but as Albert was the only baron she knew, she wasn't sure.

Albert's brushlike hair stuck out in wisps under his cap, but he was grinning happily and seemed to think he was the very image of a baron.

He tiptoed over to where Meg was standing in the dark by the pear tree, and said in an excited whisper, "Now we'll see if we've managed to fool the old man into thinking it's twelve o'clock."

"Yes, w-we'll see," Meg quavered. "Did you put the alarm clock in the laundry?"

"Of course I did. I set it, too, so the old man won't oversleep. He isn't used to getting up at this hour."

A little worn path led to the laundry down by the river. Albert turned his flashlight on so Meg wouldn't bump into one of the old mossy apple trees. Albert was always thoughtful and kind.

"May I hold your hand?" Meg asked him. "I can see better then."

"Can you?" said Albert. "That's funny." He took Meg's cold hand and felt it trembling a little.

"But when the old man comes, I'll have to let go of you," he said. "He doesn't think it's proper for me to associate with you, because you don't have any blue blood in your veins."

In the pitch blackness the laundry looked very much like a place ghosts would live in. There was a spooky silence about it. Could it really be the same merry place that was so full of pleasant noises when Mrs. Nilsson was there doing the laundry? There was always a great splashing of water when Mrs. Nilsson was throwing the clothes into the huge boilers and slapping them with the beater. The whole laundry was so full of steam that Meg and Betsy could hardly see each other as they wandered around the boilers. It was fun to be in the laundry, but the best place of all was the attic above it. Sometimes they played hide-and-seek up there and ran around and jumped and shouted as much as they pleased. There were owls nesting under the eaves, and they didn't like it at all when Meg and Betsy made a rumpus. They would fly out through the attic windows and not come back until Meg and Betsy had gone. Perhaps ghosts did the same thing. Maybe Baron Crow had also flown out through an attic window every time Meg and Betsy had been noisy there. But now he was probably sitting in the dark with the owls and brooding—brooding and waiting. Meg held tight to Albert's hand; she was afraid, and he could feel it. He turned off his flashlight and put his hand on the big heavy key, ready to turn it; then he hesitated.

"Tell me what you would like," he said. "I thought you might like to see a ghost, but you don't have to if you don't want to."

Just then they heard the alarm clock go off in the laundry,

as if it were trying to announce Meg's arrival and wake up all the ghosts. It was an awful sound.

"You can go home if you like," said Albert, "because it will take a while before Grandfather's grandfather is fully awake."

Meg was trembling with fright, but how would she ever know whether she was clairvoyant if she didn't take this chance to find out?

"I *want* to see them," she mumbled, "but just for a second."

"Well, then," said Albert, "don't blame me if you get so scared you pass out."

He turned the key, and the door slowly opened with a bloodcurdling creak that would certainly have wakened Baron Crow if by any chance he hadn't heard the alarm clock.

Meg stared into the blackness and grabbed hold of Albert's sweater. Without him she would be lost, and she knew it. "Turn on the flashlight so we can see," she pleaded.

But Albert didn't turn on the flashlight. "You're not very used to seeing ghosts, that's sure. Nothing makes them madder than having a flashlight pointed at them. It makes them growl. Have you ever heard a ghost growl?"

Fortunately, Meg never had.

"You're lucky," said Albert. "I know someone who did, and he's still shaking."

Meg now realized what a terrible mistake it would be to turn a flashlight on Baron Crow and make him growl.

Albert knew best, and she followed him into the pitch darkness without any further objection. Albert closed the door behind him, and they couldn't see a thing. Baron Crow was probably standing in the midst of the blackness, waiting for them, and he'd be terrifying enough even if he wasn't growling. They stood motionless just inside the door, waiting. Meg pressed closer to Albert.

Then Meg felt Albert stiffen and heard him catch his breath.

"There he comes, there, over by the wall."

Meg screamed and clutched Albert. She huddled against him and closed her eyes.

"Do you see him?" Albert whispered.

Meg opened her eyes reluctantly and looked in the direction of the wall. She couldn't see a thing, only blackness. Albert was probably right, she wasn't any more clairvoyant than a pig, and at that moment she was thankful for it.

"Don't you really see him?" whispered Albert. "Don't you see a white, nasty-looking thing with a sort of halo around it?"

"No," said Meg truthfully.

"That's strange," said Albert. There was no doubt that Albert could see him clearly, and talk to him too.

"Right Honorable Baron, where have you hidden the money? Answer me—that is, if you want to."

But there was no sound. The Baron evidently didn't want to answer.

"He's stubborn, as usual," Albert whispered to Meg and added in a loud voice, "I'm a baron myself and could use the money. Please, Grandfather's Grandfather, we're relatives, after all!"

Then he whispered to Meg again, "Can't you really see him? He looks just awful."

"No," Meg insisted. "I guess I'm not clairvoyant."

"Don't be so sure," said Albert. "Sometimes it can take quite a while before you get started. And then, one, two, three, you see ghosts all over the place."

But Meg was positive that she wasn't clairvoyant, and now that she was quite sure, the only thing she wanted was to get out of the laundry. Albert stiffened again and whispered, "Look, he's beckoning to me, he wants me to come. Yes, Grandfather's Grandfather, I'm coming."

But Meg clung to him. "Please don't leave me," she whispered, terrified.

"I have to," whispered Albert. "He wants to show me where the money is. Stay here. Don't move."

Suddenly Meg was alone in the dark. She heard Albert tiptoe across the floor and didn't know what to do. She didn't dare try to follow him, and she didn't dare to stay where she was.

"Albert," she called, "Albert!"

But Albert didn't answer. He had disappeared into the darkness. The seconds went by, and he didn't come back. They were very long seconds for Meg.

Meg in her arms and sat down on the kitchen sofa, rocking her gently.

"Alva, I've seen a ghost," Meg whispered. "Oh, Alva, I'm *clairvoyant!*"

It was some time before Alva could get anything more out of her. She was in such a state that she could hardly talk—and besides, Albert had said she mustn't tell a living soul. But she had to tell *someone,* and finally Alva heard the whole story about Baron Crow in the Nilssons' laundry. She flew into a rage.

"I'm going to scalp that Albert! He's going to catch it! Him and his ghosts!"

But Meg defended him. "He can't help being clairvoyant."

"Oh, can't he!" said Alva, furiously. "Just wait till I've finished with him! Then he won't be clairvoyant any longer, I promise you. The Right Honorable Albert, indeed!"

Fortunately Mother and Father were asleep, and Alva promised Meg to tell them nothing. "If your mother hears about this, you've been to the Nilssons' for the last time. But I'm going to give Albert a talking to that he won't forget."

The next day, when Meg came home from school, Albert was leaning on the fence as if he were waiting for someone. He still had his hair, so Alva hadn't scalped him. But she must have given him a piece of her mind, because he looked very shamefaced.

He whistled, and Meg went over to him. "I had no idea

"Albert," she wailed, "Albert, I want to go ho

But then she saw something. Oh, horror, she
voyant after all! She saw a white, terrible thing w.
of halo around it. Baron Crow was standing over
wall, as sure as anything.

Then Meg screamed as she had never screamed i
life—screamed and screamed and groped for the door, t₁
to get out. The light around Baron Crow went out, and
couldn't see him any more, but still she went on screamii
Albert's voice came out of the darkness.

"Quiet, Meg, don't scream like that! You're frightening
Baron Crow."

But Meg didn't hear a word. She was frantic and all she
wanted was to get out—out!

Alva had come back from town, where she had spent the
evening, and she was just about to put the key in the kitchen
door when Meg came racing across the lawn. Without a
word she threw her arms around Alva so violently that Alva
was almost knocked over.

"What on earth are you doing out at this time of night?"
Alva asked.

Meg only moaned, and Alva could feel her whole body
trembling. Alva didn't ask any more questions but quickly
led Meg into the kitchen and turned on the light. It wasn't
easy, because Meg was clinging to her as if she were
drowning.

"What on earth has happened?" Alva asked. She took

that you were that clairvoyant," he said, "or I never would have taken you along to the laundry."

Meg shuddered at the mention of the laundry. "I'm never going there again."

"Why not?" Albert asked her. "You don't have to be afraid of Grandfather's Grandfather. He won't come any more."

"How do you know?" asked Meg in astonishment.

"Because he is through with being a ghost. I've dug up the money."

"You have?" said Meg.

"Yes, but it's a secret, so don't go and tell Alva."

Feeling ashamed, Meg promised not to tell. She looked curiously at Albert. "Are you rich now?"

Albert spat thoughtfully on the ground. "Well, I think that Grandfather's Grandfather has made an awful lot of fuss for only two-fifty." He put his hand in his pocket and pulled out the money.

"Was that all?" asked Meg.

"Yes, that was all. But remember that Grandfather's Grandfather lived more than a hundred years ago, and at that time two-fifty was not to be sneezed at, so no wonder he's been hanging around." Albert put a fifty-cent piece in Meg's hand. "Here, this is for your mental anguish, or whatever it's called."

Meg beamed. Albert *was* nice, after all. "Thank you, Albert. You're awfully kind."

"You're welcome. It's ghost money, but it's just as good as ordinary money."

Then the Right Honorable Albert disappeared into his kitchen. Meg was left standing there, very pleased with her ghost money.

"Just think, it's been buried in Nilssons' laundry over a hundred years, but still it's shiny and looks real."

Yes, it looked exactly the way a coin should. She decided to spend it on paper dolls.

CHAPTER VI

Now the Snowstorms Start Their Journey

Now the long winter darkness had settled over June Hill. Christmas would soon be here. Meg and Betsy talked about it every night.

"I'm so glad there's such a thing as Christmas," Meg said. "I think it's the best thing that was ever invented."

"Ab-so-lute-ly," said Betsy.

They shook their piggy banks, which sounded as if they had a lot of money in them. All that jingling would turn into Christmas presents, and that is why it sounded so good.

A calendar hung on the wall in their room, and every morning they tore off a page, which brought them one day closer to Christmas.

At school, too, you could tell that Christmas was near. The teacher told Christmas stories, and everybody learned Christmas songs. Meg sang them for Betsy at home.

> Now the snowstorms start their journey
> Through the mountains and the valleys in the north.

All of a sudden, the holidays had come. "Oh, why do we have to have holidays?" That's what Meg had said the first day of school, a long time ago. But after a whole term, she thought that holidays were almost as good an idea as Christmas itself.

Alva and Ida had begun the Christmas preparations by taking down all the curtains to be washed. There were scrubbing pails in the most unexpected places, and Alva went around with a long brush, dusting walls and ceilings. Meg and Betsy wandered around the pails and got in the way wherever they went. They teased Alva by singing, "Now Alva starts her journey round the walls and round the ceilings." Betsy giggled so she almost fell into a pail. "Oh, what good songs you invent, Meggie," she said.

But Alva chased them with a brush, saying, "Now this brush starts its journey, and there are going to be spankings in the north." But she wasn't really angry. She never was angry with Meg and Betsy.

Mother was making sausages, curing ham, dipping candles, and preparing a Christmas drink of juniper berries. Meg and Betsy were allowed to help in the kitchen. They baked gingerbread men, made butterscotch, molded little pigs of marzipan, and cut crepe paper for the decorations around the stove. Every day was filled with excitement, and every day felt more and more like Christmas. It even *smelled* like Christmas—the most wonderful smell of gingerbread and butterscotch and cookies all over the house. Several times a day Meg would close her eyes and blissfully breathe in the fragrance.

At night they wrote long lists of things they wanted Santa Claus to bring. *"Robinson Crusoe,* lots of paper dolls, tin soldiers, skis, a light red rose to wear in my hair," were the items on one of Meg's lists, which she read to Betsy.

"Do you really want a rose?" Betsy asked.

"Not exactly," said Meg. "I just wrote it because it sounds so pretty."

They thought very carefully what they should give Mother and Father. While they were helping Mother make the butterscotch, Meg asked, "Mother, what do you wish for most of all?"

"Two very good little girls," Mother replied.

Suddenly there was a strange expression in Meg's eyes, and her voice quivered a little. "What will you do with Betsy and me, then?"

Mother stroked her hair and explained that she didn't

want any *other* little girls, she just wanted Meg and Betsy to keep on being as good as they had always been.

But Betsy didn't think it would be such a bad idea to have some new girls in the house. "We could play with them," she said. "But they couldn't live in our room, because that belongs to Meg and me."

The weather was beginning to be very cold, and every morning Alva lighted a fire in the children's room. She rattled and banged with the shutters of the porcelain stove, and the noise awakened Meg and Betsy. Then they lay in bed and watched the flames through the little openings in the shutters, and listened to the fire crackle. It was a good, pleasant sound to wake up to.

One morning they woke up earlier than usual, thinking it was an ordinary day. But far from it! It was the last Sunday in Advent, and four candles were burning in the candlesticks on the table. Alva, who had just lighted the fire, was standing beside Meg's bed, looking mysterious.

"Something strange happened last night," she said. "Can you guess what?"

"A ghost?" said Meg. Ever since her adventure in the Nilssons' laundry, she'd had the notion that the really mysterious things that happen at night are sure to be ghosts.

"Silly, there's no such thing as a ghost," said Alva. "I've told you it was only Albert dressed up in a sheet and shining the flashlight on himself."

Alva had told Meg this over and over again, but Meg didn't

believe her. Albert could never do a thing like that—someone else, maybe, but not Albert.

"Guess again," said Alva. "It's something very nice."

"Ghosts are nice," said Betsy.

"I don't think so at all," Alva said firmly. "Take another guess."

"Do we have snow?" asked Meg eagerly.

"No," said Alva, "but the river is frozen over!"

Meg and Betsy gave a shout of joy and jumped out of bed. The room wasn't warm yet, but they were in such a hurry they didn't care. They scrambled into their clothes, put on woolen leggings and heavy sweaters, hoods and gloves, and dashed outside.

"Only for a few minutes," Alva called after them. "You have to come back and have your breakfast soon."

"All right," Meg and Betsy shouted back over their shoulders.

The birches around June Hill were white with frost, and the sun was a fiery red ball over the woodshed.

"I love this kind of weather!" said Meg.

She really liked all kinds of weather, but mostly she hardly even noticed it; it was just there. But this was the kind of weather that made you take notice. It was beautiful in the way that songs and their words are beautiful, Meg thought. It made her want to be especially good.

As she and Betsy ran down to the river the frosty, stiff grass crunched under their feet.

"Maybe I'll even give you two Christmas presents, Betsy."
Meg panted as she ran.

"You're crazy, Meggie," said Betsy. Of course she was
pleased about the possibility of getting two presents, but at
the moment all she was really interested in was the ice. It
was thrilling to take your first step on the shiny dark ice to
test how slippery it was. The river was so slippery that Meg
took a long slide that carried her almost to the opposite
side. It wasn't entirely true that all this ice had come over-
night. The weather had been freezing for a whole week, but
Meg and Betsy hadn't noticed how the river was becoming
smoother and smoother every day. Only Alva had noticed it,
and that morning, before anyone else was awake, she had
gone down to test the ice with a heavy pole.

"No one has to be afraid to walk on it, because if it will
hold Alva, it will hold us," Meg said.

"Ab-so-lute-ly," said Betsy.

Meg and Betsy had a wonderful time gliding and sliding.
Their cheeks were red and their breath came out like white
smoke. They couldn't understand how people could stay in
bed on a day like this. But in Peaceful Villa no one seemed
to be awake. Albert evidently didn't know that the whole
river was like a smooth, shiny road to slide on. Around every
bend there were new stretches of fine ice to explore. If you
passed Peaceful Villa and kept going, you came eventually to
Apple Lake, where there was real country, and a real farm
called Apple Hill.

"Maybe we ought to go and say hello to the Petrus Karlssons at Apple Hill," Meg suggested.

"Do you think Mother would let us?" Betsy asked.

Mother was still sleeping—after all, it was Sunday morning, and they couldn't wake her up just to ask such a silly question.

"Of course she'd let us," said Meg. "Not if we were to take the road, of course, because that would take too long, but if we slide there on the ice, it will take us no time at all."

"All right," said Betsy.

Neither of them remembered what Alva had said about breakfast, so they started merrily gliding along in the direction of Apple Hill.

"Ice is something I really like," said Meg.

"Everyone likes ice," said Betsy.

But Meg didn't just like the ice; it made her feel so happy that her heart danced with joy. This long, wide road of ice was like a miracle. The winter river and the summer river were entirely different. Sometimes on a summer evening they rowed with Father all the way to Apple Hill to buy eggs, and then it was a gentle little river, flowing quietly along between green trees. Soft green branches hung out over the water so that Meg and Betsy could touch the leaves from their seats in the boat.

But the winter river seemed to be enchanted. The glossy dark ice and the strange red sun, making the frosty white trees sparkle, were beautiful in a cold and fairy-like way that thrilled Meg. The faster she went sliding along, the more lighthearted she became. She felt almost as if she were flying to Heaven.

Betsy was behind. "Wait for me," she shouted.

She was beginning to be tired of sliding, and now she settled down to walk, and not very fast at that. Meg had to stop and wait until Betsy caught up with her.

"How far is it to Apple Hill?" Betsy asked suspiciously.

"Not far at all," Meg assured her. "We'll soon be there."

"Take my hand," Betsy said and tucked her fist into Meg's. They went trudging along, hand in hand, quite slowly now, expecting to see the lake and Apple Hill Farm behind every new bend. But there was only the river stretching ahead of them.

Betsy had had enough. "Meg, do you know what? I'm hungry."

Then they suddenly remembered Alva saying, "You have to come back and have your breakfast soon."

And there they were, cold and tired and far from home. They looked at each other in dismay. Meg realized that she too was very hungry, but she didn't want to turn back. It could be only a little farther to Apple Hill, and it would be wonderful to rest there for a while.

"We can each buy an egg from Mrs. Karlsson," she said, "and ask them to cook it so we can eat it right away."

"Do we have any money?" asked Betsy.

"No," said Meg. But then she remembered that the day

before she had put two cents into the pocket of the checkered skirt she was wearing, and she began to feel around for the coins.

"Can you get two eggs for two cents?" asked Betsy.

Meg was doubtful. "I don't think so, but we can try. We'll say that we want two cents' worth of eggs, and then we'll see what happens."

But unfortunately she didn't find the two cents.

"What are we going to do now?" Betsy asked.

Meg shrugged her shoulders. "Well, two cents more or less can't make much difference when you're buying eggs."

Betsy didn't think it could either.

"Let's go anyway," said Meg. "Mrs. Karlsson may invite us for breakfast and we'll say, 'yes, thank you,' right away."

The thought of breakfast around the next bend put new life into them. They went sliding along again for a while, then walked for a bit, but *still* they were not within sight of Apple Hill.

"Perhaps they put the farm someplace else during the winter," Betsy suggested.

"Don't be silly," said Meg, but she too was beginning to wonder. "This is very strange. If we don't see Apple Hill when we come to that bend, it'll mean we're bewitched, and if that's the case, I feel sorry for us."

Meg couldn't shake off the idea of witchcraft. The trees were so beautiful and lifeless with their white frosty branches; only in bewitched forests do trees look like that.

The dark glossy ice, which could make children lose their heads and lure them a long way from home, might be a bewitched road without end. Little ghostly winter witches probably flew around there at night. Yes, it must be witch-craft; there could be no other explanation.

But Betsy didn't want to be bewitched, she said, sobbing miserably.

And then, just as they trudged round the bend, what should they see but Apple Hill, with its barn and its stable and its cozy red farmhouse!

Betsy stopped crying at once. "Apple Hill is a lovely farm," she said cheerfully.

Meg heartily agreed. "I hope they're home," she said, "especially Tore and Maja."

Tore and Maja were the Apple Hill children, and Meg was fond of them, although they were terribly old—almost twenty.

Meg and Betsy couldn't have come at a more suitable time. Everyone was sitting at the breakfast table—Petrus Karls-son, Mrs. Karlsson, Tore, and Maja—when they walked in, like two red-cheeked Christmas angels.

"Do you have any eggs for sale?" asked Betsy before any-one else had a chance to say a word. Meg pinched her. Silly Betsy, what a stupid thing to say! It would have been all right if they'd had any money, but as it was, they couldn't pay a cent.

"My dears, did you come all this way in the cold just to

buy eggs?" asked Mrs. Karlsson. "How many eggs does your mother want?"

Meg and Betsy were embarrassed. They didn't know how to explain that Mother hadn't sent them at all. Meg was furious with Betsy. She'd spoiled everything. People who came to buy eggs wouldn't be invited to have breakfast; only those who had come to visit would be invited.

"We're really only out for a walk," said Meg at last.

And Betsy added, "Because we have no money, we're out for a walk without any money."

"Oh," said Mr. Karlsson, stirring his coffee. "Yes, it's wonderful weather to be out walking in—without any money."

"Yes, wonderful," Meg agreed. "It gives you such an appetite."

"Yes, I'm sure it does," said Mr. Karlsson, but it didn't seem as if he understood very well.

Mrs. Karlsson understood better. "May I give you some breakfast?" she asked.

"Yes, thank you!" said Meg and Betsy in unison.

They quickly took off their hoods and sweaters and gloves, and before Maja had time to get plates for them, they were sitting down at the table.

When the Karlssons had finished their breakfast they stayed at the table just to talk to Betsy and Meg.

"So you're out taking a walk?" said Mr. Karlsson, laughing.

By this time Meg and Betsy had their mouths so full that they couldn't answer, so they only nodded. Mrs. Karlsson had given them huge slices of bread and butter, which they were hungrily devouring with their porridge. It wasn't hard to see that the weather had given them an appetite.

"I love porridge," said Meg. "Don't you, Betsy?"

"No," said Betsy. She certainly *liked* porridge, and especially right now, but she didn't *love* porridge, and she always said exactly what she meant.

The Karlssons laughed. They had a special laugh. Everyone at Apple Hill laughed in the same way, quietly and kindly.

"Well, what do you love, then?" asked Mrs. Karlsson.

Betsy thought for a moment. "Gooseberry pudding, and pudding . . . and other pudding."

The Karlssons laughed again. "Gooseberry pudding, and pudding . . . and other pudding," said Mrs. Karlsson. "That's an awful lot of pudding."

Meg was the only one who understood what Betsy meant. "Gooseberry pudding is gooseberry pudding, and pudding is apple pudding, and other pudding is all other kinds of pudding," she explained.

It was Tore's turn to laugh. "Gooseberry pudding and other pudding. Is that all you eat at June Hill?"

"No, it isn't," said Betsy, annoyed. "We eat ice cream. On my fifth birthday Mother let me eat all the ice cream I wanted, at least ten pounds."

"Oh," said Mrs. Karlsson, "so you're five already! When were you five?"

"Oh, she doesn't know that herself," said Meg.

Betsy scowled at her. "Don't I? I most certainly do."

"You do? When was it?"

"On my birthday—there," said Betsy and stuck out her tongue at Meg. Meg stuck out her tongue right back at Betsy, and then they remembered that you don't behave like that when you're a guest. They thanked the Karlssons very politely, going around the table to shake hands, and curtsying to Mr. Karlsson, Mrs. Karlsson, Tore, and Maja. Now they weren't hungry any longer, but they were terribly tired. It was nice to sit in the warm kitchen, and they didn't feel at all like going out into the cold again.

"I think I'd better telephone your father," Mr. Karlsson said. "Perhaps they don't know at home that you're here buying eggs—without any money."

Meg and Betsy were terribly ashamed of themselves and listened uneasily while Mr. Karlsson called up June Hill. Meg stood beside him and tugged at his sleeve. "Ask if we may stay for a while and rest."

Mr. Karlsson did so and added, "I'll drive them home soon."

Meg and Betsy looked pleased, but then Mr. Karlsson handed the receiver to Meg. "Your father wants to talk to you," he said, and the smile disappeared from Meg's face.

"Listen to me, my girl," said Father sternly, "how would

it be if you used your head for a change? Going so far in this cold! Just suppose you'd got your noses frozen off, what would you say then?"

Meg kept on thinking about that after she had hung up the telephone receiver. Was it really possible to have your nose frozen off? How terrible if, while she was walking along with Betsy, their noses had suddenly dropped off and landed on the ice, like two little cold pieces of leather. What *would* they have said then? "Good-by, noses," maybe. Meg shuddered at the thought and was just about to start crying over her lost nose when she suddenly remembered that both she and Betsy still had their noses. Thank goodness!

Betsy was using hers right then, burrowing it into Tore's thick jacket, which was hanging over a chair. "It smells so good," she said. "It smells like the barnyard. Can we go there?"

Tore was just as nice as his father. "Yes, of course we can," he said, laughing in that quiet, amusing way, just as if he knew a funny secret.

He took them down to the barnyard and showed them the big bull and all the cows and calves. There was a newborn calf in a pen, and the girls were delighted with him. Although he could hardly stand on his legs, he came to the barrier and put his wet muzzle against Meg and Betsy. They held out their fingers for him to lick, and Meg told him that, in case he didn't know it, it would soon be Christmas.

Then Tore took them to the stables and showed them the

four horses, Titus, Mona, Freja, and Konke. Meg and Betsy
had seen them last in the summer, when they were out in the
meadow. But now they were standing in their stalls and
they neighed a greeting when Meg and Betsy came in.

Konke was the friendliest one, but the ugliest. His coat
was a queer yellow color.

"It doesn't matter how you look, though, as long as you're
good," said Meg.

They went into his stall and patted him on the back,
brushed him, and fed him some oats. Tore chuckled quietly
to himself as he stood watching them.

"Which manger did little Jesus lie in?" Betsy asked suddenly. As far as she knew, the Apple Hill stable was the
only one in the world.

Meg explained to her that it was in an entirely different
stable, far away in Bethlehem.

"How do you know?" asked Betsy.

"I know because the teacher said so."

Betsy wasn't at all pleased. "No, he was lying in Konke's
manger. That is what they said in my school. And Konke
was so good to him and didn't bite him, just sniffed a little
at him to find out who he was."

Meg looked around the shadowy stable. She too would
have liked Jesus' manger to be at Apple Hill.

"Perhaps it was here, after all," she said eagerly. "And
Mary put lights in all the windows, and Mr. Karlsson and
Mrs. Karlsson sat in the kitchen and saw the light shining

across the snow, and then Mrs. Karlsson said, 'Who do you suppose is in the stable tonight?'"

Betsy knew the answer to that. "It is only little Jesus," she said. "He is lying in Konke's manger, and Konke is sniffing at him, and Jesus is laughing. He likes that."

"Am I sitting in the kitchen too, looking out at the light in the stable?" Tore asked.

"Now you're being pretty silly, Tore," said Meg. "This happened ages ago when you weren't even born."

While they were in the stable the weather had changed. The red sun had disappeared behind dark clouds, and snowflakes were flying through the air.

"Hooray, it's beginning to snow," said Meg.

Soon the snow was falling heavily over Apple Hill. "I can't drive you home in weather like this," Mr. Karlsson said. "We'll have to wait until it stops."

"Yes, let's," said Meg and Betsy both at once. They didn't at all mind waiting until the snowstorm was over. Maja still had all the dolls she had played with when she was a little girl, and she brought them out. Meg and Betsy lined them up on the kitchen sofa, changed their clothes, and had a wonderful time.

Outside, the snow was still falling steadily.

"This will probably turn into a sleigh ride," said Mr. Karlsson, "but we'll wait until it stops."

"Yes, please," said Meg and Betsy, who were very happy playing with the dolls.

Suddenly Mrs. Karlsson called Betsy. "Which do you really like best?" she asked. "Gooseberry pudding or other pudding or just plain pudding?"

"Gooseberry pudding," Betsy said promptly.

"You're lucky, because that's exactly what we're having for dessert, and not pudding or other pudding," said Mrs. Karlsson. "Come now, let's have dinner!"

They sat down to a wonderful meal of ham with onion sauce and gooseberry pudding with milk. The snow was still falling.

"It looks as if it would never stop," said Mr. Karlsson. "Maybe we'd better get going anyway, or they'll think at June Hill that we've decided to keep you."

"Perhaps it will stop soon," said Mrs. Karlsson. "You'd better wait a while."

But the snow kept on falling. There were tall white hoods on the gateposts, and the flakes were coming down so thickly that you could hardly see the barn from the kitchen window. Soon it began to get dark.

"Tore, you'll have to hitch up the horses to the snowplow," said Mr. Karlsson, "or I'll never get to June Hill with these two youngsters."

Tore harnessed Mona and Freja to the snowplow, and Mr. Karlsson harnessed Titus and Konke to the sleigh. Meg and Betsy were tucked under a fur rug in the sleigh so that only their noses stuck out and they couldn't even wave good-by to Mrs. Karlsson and Maja, who were standing in the window to watch them leave. Mr. Karlsson drove the sleigh, while Tore drove the snowplow on ahead.

"Imagine it taking four horses to get us back to June Hill!" said Meg.

"Four horses *and* a snowplow," said Betsy. "That's almost a sleigh party."

They pretended that they were on a sleigh party and curled up under the fur rug, listening to the bells on the horses' collars—for they were driving back to June Hill to the sound of four sleigh bells!

"I'm certainly glad we went to Apple Hill," Meg said.

"But it still doesn't look as if it would ever stop snowing," said Mr. Karlsson. He probably wasn't nearly as comfortable up in the driver's seat as Meg and Betsy were down under the fur rug.

"We can sing for him and cheer him up a little," whispered Meg to Betsy.

"Oh, Christmastime," sang Meg.

"Oh, joyful season," Betsy chimed in just as they came to the gate of June Hill.

"Look, there are four lights burning in the window!" Betsy exclaimed.

"Yes," said Meg, "because it's Advent, don't you remember?"

CHAPTER VII

Christmas at June Hill

"So," said Alva the night before Christmas Eve. "Now everything is ready. I'm tired out, but thank goodness I've finished everything in time!"

"Except for the Christmas tree," Betsy reminded her. "Because Mother and Father are going to trim it tonight while we're sleeping."

Meg didn't say anything. She just curled up and shivered with delight the way she always did when everything was so wonderful she could hardly stand it.

Now Christmas could come to June Hill, because everything was ready. Every piece of furniture was polished, every corner scrubbed, and every window had white, newly starched curtains. There were candles in all the candlesticks, and new rag rugs in the kitchen, the copper pans were gleaming on the wall, and the kitchen range was decorated with red and green crepe paper, looking as festive as Christmas itself. The living room was fragrant with the white hyacinths that Mother had grown in time for Christmas, and the tree smelled green and fresh as it stood waiting to be trimmed.

"We have enough food to last until next Christmas," said Alva. Meg and Betsy had been inspecting the pantry, and they thought so too. On the big table the Christmas ham was competing with the head cheese, the spareribs with the liverwurst, anchovy salad, and meat balls.

Hanging from the ceiling were rows of bologna and sausage. The juniper-berry juice was in its jug, the Christmas fish in its basin, the cheesecake in its box—everything was ready. Loaves of bread and saffron rolls were stacked in the breadbox, gingerbread and almond cake and all kinds of cookies filled the cooky tins. Tonight Father would place sheaves of wheat in the apple trees so the sparrows would know when they woke up that Christmas had come.

Alva put wood in front of all the fireplaces and shoveled small winding paths to the gate, the woodshed, and the river. The river was very important because that was the way Santa Claus would come, and Betsy and Meg knew it would be a disaster if he couldn't get through all the snow. He wouldn't have any trouble this year, though, because the whole river was clear, thanks to Tore, who had driven his snowplow all the way back to Apple Hill on Advent Sunday, after returning Meg and Betsy to June Hill. That would make things easy for Santa Claus on Christmas Eve.

Albert too was grateful to Tore for plowing the river, for

he had made himself a sled, much to the delight of Meg and Betsy, especially when he gave them rides on it. He whirled them around so fast that they got dizzy.

But Albert couldn't get away from his baking very often; his pretzels were too much in demand for Christmas. Mrs. Nilsson sold them at the market every day. What Mr. Nilsson did, no one knew, but he seemed to be very busy. At any rate he was hardly ever at home.

The night before Christmas Eve, Meg went over to Peaceful Villa to see what Albert was doing. She found him on his knees scrubbing the kitchen floor, but he stopped as soon as Meg came in.

"I was just going to clean up a little," he explained. He had already scrubbed half the floor, and it was easy to see where he had worked, for the scrubbed part was not nearly as black as the unscrubbed part. Meg looked around. Except for the floor, there hadn't been much Christmas housecleaning done at Peaceful Villa. The curtains and the embroidered covers on the shelves had not been washed. Everything looked the same as usual, and it shouldn't be the same as usual the night before Christmas Eve. Meg felt very strongly about this.

"Aren't you ready yet?" she asked.

Albert looked surprised. "Ready for what?"

Meg didn't exactly know what to answer. "Well, it's Christmas Eve tomorrow."

"Oh, yes, we're ready," said Albert. "Come and see!"

He went ahead of Meg into the little room next to the kitchen and showed her a paper streamer decorated with bearded Santa Clauses, nailed up on the wall.

"What do you say to that?" he asked triumphantly. "Mother and Dad haven't seen it yet. It is a surprise for them."

Meg still wasn't satisfied. "Don't you have a Christmas tree?" she asked.

"While there's life, there's hope," said Albert. "Maybe Dad will bring one when he comes home tonight—that is, if he hasn't forgotten. In that case I'll go out and chop one down in the woods tomorrow morning, because I'm going to have a Christmas tree."

Then Meg thought of her tree at June Hill, and one of those little shivers of joy raced through her. "Isn't Christmas wonderful, Albert?"

"Yes, it's nice to fix the place up for Christmas. I like that streamer."

Meg liked the streamer with the bearded Santa Clauses too, but it decorated only one little spot, and Meg wanted Christmas to be all over the place. But Albert probably wasn't that particular.

"Do you think you'll get a lot of Christmas presents?" she asked.

"While there's life, there's hope," Albert said again. "I hope Mother and Dad haven't forgotten. But do you want to see what I've bought? Swear that you won't tell a single living soul?"

Meg promised. Then Albert carefully opened the door to the closet and pointed proudly to a brand-new lamp with a white lampshade. It looked expensive and elegant.

"That's an improvement on the junky one we have now," said Albert.

"Is it going to be a Christmas present?" Meg asked.

"Yes, I'm going to give it to Mother and Dad, and they can call it a Christmas present or whatever they like," said Albert. "It's very expensive, and I earned every penny for it myself."

Meg went home, deep in thought. Both the lamp and the bearded Santa Clauses were all right, but still they made her anxious to get back to June Hill. It was hard to believe that it really would be Christmas tomorrow when she was at Peaceful Villa, and this bothered her. She talked to Betsy about it when they went to bed.

"Suppose it isn't Christmas Eve tomorrow when we wake up, but just Friday?"

"Then I'll drown myself," said Betsy. She had heard Alva say that sometimes, and Betsy was quick to pick up such expressions.

But Betsy didn't have to drown herself. It was Christmas Eve when they woke up. It was still dark outside, but Father came into their room with lighted candles and they could hear Mother playing "Christmas Is Here Again" on the piano downstairs.

"Yes, Christmas is here again," said Father. "Merry Christmas, my little girls."

"Merry Christmas, Father," cried Meg and Betsy as they flew out of bed and dashed downstairs into the living room. There was the tree, all lit up and more beautiful than they remembered a Christmas tree could be. There was a fire in the porcelain stove, and the room was fragrant with the smell of the Christmas tree, firewood, and hyacinth. Christmas had really come!

For a moment they stood speechless, but they quickly recovered. They ran across the floor, leaping with joy, jumping, dancing, and singing, while Sasso barked. Christmas had really come!

Then Alva brought in the breakfast tray, and they all sat in front of the fire, Mother, Father, Alva, Meg, and Betsy. Meg and Betsy considered it a special treat to have breakfast in their pajamas. "It's because it's Christmas," Betsy said.

"Yes, because it's Christmas," said Mother.

Meg looked anxiously at Mother to see if she was tired, but fortunately Mother was happy and not at all tired. Everyone had to be happy, and everyone had to feel that Christmas was wonderful, or something was spoiled for Meg. She had kept on saying to Mother, when she was working on the Christmas preparations, "You have to promise not to be tired on Christmas Eve."

"Now, how *could* I be tired on Christmas Eve?" Mother had asked.

Sitting here with Father and Alva, she seemed to be just as happy about Christmas as Meg and Betsy. Oh, how wonderful it all was!

It began to get lighter outside, and the sparrows were awake and eating their breakfast in the sheaves of wheat. Meg and Betsy watched them through the living-room window.

"Do sparrows know it's Christmas, Father?" Betsy wondered.

"Perhaps they don't," said Father, "but I think they understand what Christmas sheaves are."

"I understand *everything*," Betsy said.

But there was one thing neither Meg nor Betsy could understand. Why should Christmas Eve be twice as long as any other day in the year? Who decided that? Mother did what she could to make the long hours go a little faster. First she sent Meg and Betsy to Ida with the traditional Christmas basket. Ida had to share their Christmas ham, and the head cheese and the spareribs and sausage and liverwurst and bread and cake and coffee and cookies and apples and candles. Mother packed everything into the red basket, and then Meg and Betsy took it and started off in the cold to Ida's house.

Ida lived all alone in her little house. Her girls had gone far away to America. As Meg stood on the doorstep, she was suddenly worried. Maybe Christmas didn't mean so much to Ida.

But she needn't have worried. Ida was sitting in her wicker chair in front of the fireplace, looking very contented, with her feet in a basin of warm water. "Both my feet and I know it's Christmas. For three wonderful days we're going to sit here doing absolutely nothing."

She was delighted with the Christmas basket and immediately had to taste the liverwurst and the head cheese. She gave the bologna an approving pat.

"But this is all wrong," she said. "You bring me all the food you can carry, and I sit here like a queen, soaking my feet and stuffing myself."

They couldn't stay very long at Ida's because it was time to go home and dip bread in the soup-kettle, as they always did on Christmas Eve.

"Merry Christmas, Ida!" cried Meg and Betsy. And Ida, with her feet in the basin and a piece of ham in her hand, looked as if she really would have a Merry Christmas.

Christmas Eve crawled forward, bit by bit. Meg and Betsy dipped bread in the kettle, not because they thought bread dipped in broth tasted particularly good but because it was a tradition and it was fun to have everybody in the kitchen together, all dipping their pieces of bread into the same kettle.

"You *have* to do it, because otherwise it isn't Christmas," said Meg.

During the next few hours they busily wrapped Christmas presents. Father helped them to put red sealing wax on all the packages. But entirely without Father's help, Betsy put a little hot sealing wax on her thumb, and her screams could be heard all over the house.

"Wax shouldn't be allowed," she said bitterly when she had finished screaming.

"Wax certainly should be allowed," Meg said, "or otherwise it wouldn't smell like Christmas."

She talked to Betsy about how wonderful it would be if they could hide a little of the wax smell in a jar together with all the other good Christmas smells. Then they could keep the jar to sniff at all year, until Christmas came again.

Among Meg's presents was a little package for Albert containing a small harmonica. She had bought it with the ghost money she got after the night in the Nilssons' laundry.

Usually she and Albert didn't exchange Christmas presents, but she was terribly afraid that he wouldn't get very many and that he would be unhappy. When it began to get dark, she ran down to Peaceful Villa with her present, closely followed by Betsy.

The Nilssons were in the kitchen, as usual, and Mr. Nilsson was lying on the sofa, as usual. But there was an unusual lightness about the kitchen. The new lamp was shining brightly on the table, and Albert's eyes were shining even more brightly. He seemed to see nothing but the lamp and hardly even noticed Meg and Betsy. But Mr. Nilsson nodded to them from the couch in a friendly way.

"Little Meg and little Betsy from June Hill, you came just in time," he said, pointing proudly to the lamp. "What do you think of this magnificent gift my son has bought? What a difference this bright light makes!"

"Yes, it's lovely," said Meg.

"And take a look in the other room. What do you think about the funny little Santa Clauses that my son has put up on the wall? And the Christmas tree, which he got just to give his old father pleasure? Albert, you're a good son."

Mrs. Nilsson was sitting as close to the lamp as she could get, drinking coffee. She put the cup down and stroked Albert on the head. "As if he didn't do it for his mother too! Yes, you certainly are a nice boy, Albert."

Albert was embarrassed by all this praise. He turned to Meg and Betsy and said, "What do you want, anyway?"

Meg produced the package, which she had been holding behind her back. "I just wanted to give you a Christmas present," she said.

"A Christmas present for me? But why?"

Mrs. Nilsson clapped her hands together in dismay. "A Christmas present for Albert! We completely forgot!" She gave Mr. Nilsson an accusing look. "Emil, did you remember to get Albert a Christmas present, by any chance?"

Mr. Nilsson just looked sourly at Mrs. Nilsson and finally said in an annoyed tone, "Although I am a house-owner and a property-owner, I am a little short of cash at the moment. Therefore, Albert didn't get a present. Do you feel bad about that, Albert?"

Albert didn't look sad at all. "We have the lamp."

"And Meggie's Christmas present, too," Betsy reminded him.

"Yes, that's right. Meg brought me a Christmas present." He opened the package and took out the harmonica.

Mr. Nilsson was delighted. "Oh, a harmonica! That's just fine. Now you can play something nice for your old father."

It wasn't an expensive harmonica, but Albert could play on it just the same. He sat beside his lamp, playing "Christmas Is Here Again," and sounding almost all the right notes. Then he played "Home, Sweet Home," and Mr. Nilsson cried because that was his favorite song.

Meg and Betsy went back to June Hill, pleased with their visit. "It was nice in their house," said Betsy.

"Yes, it was," Meg agreed. "What a fine lamp! I would like to have one like it."

Night came at last, and all the Christmas candles were lit at June Hill. Betsy thought this was so that Santa Claus could find his way in the dark. But Santa Claus wouldn't be coming until seven o'clock. He'd called himself and said so, Father told them.

That was too bad, because it would have been nice to have him in the kitchen right then. Alva had set the big table with everything June Hill had to offer—ham, rice pudding,

Christmas fish, spareribs, sausage, meat balls, anchovy salad, and many other things. Meg and Betsy counted twenty different serving dishes. Both girls were terribly excited and had a hard time sitting still. The heat from all the candles made their cheeks glow, they talked and laughed and played like baby calves, but they didn't eat very much.

Then, when Father had lit the candles on the Christmas tree and Mother was sitting at the piano, they quieted down because now they were going to sing all the Christmas songs, and nothing could feel more like Christmas than that.

> "Shine over sea and land,
> Oh, distant star."

Meg was so happy that she felt a lump in her throat. It seemed as if the Christmas lights shone more brightly when she was singing, and as if she were a better person. She would ask Betsy to forgive her for all sorts of things, but she wasn't sure exactly what.

Suddenly Father said, "Put on your coats quickly, because Santa Claus will be here any minute."

Then they all went outside, Mother, Father, Alva, Meg, and Betsy. It was quite dark, but the ground and trees were white with snow, and the stars were bright above the roof.

Meg and Betsy took each other by the hand and ran down the little path to the river. The night was very quiet, but somewhere far away they could hear the faint sound of sleigh bells. Santa Claus was coming! They stood on the landing in the snow and heard the sleigh bells coming closer and closer. They shivered with excitement and pressed themselves close to their mother. At last they could see the glow of a torch shining across the snow at the bend of the river. Then they could see the horse and sleigh. There was Santa Claus! He was sitting in his sleigh with his white beard and his red hood, and the horse came trotting up to the landing.

"Whoa, whoa," said Santa Claus and stopped right in front of Meg and Betsy. They stood in speechless suspense, not daring to say a word, staring at Santa Claus with big round eyes. The horse also got his share of their attention— an ugly little horse, like Konke at Apple Hill. To think that there could be other horses in the world just as yellow and just as ugly!—but Konke didn't have a black pompon on his forehead, of course.

"Are there any good children here?" asked Santa Claus, and he sounded good and kind, just like Tore at Apple Hill.

Were there any good children? "Yes, there certainly are!" said Father emphatically. "Meg and Betsy are very good girls indeed."

"Well, in that case . . ." said Santa Claus and pulled a big sack out of his sleigh. "Merry Christmas!" He almost sounded a bit shy.

He tapped his ugly horse and turned the sleigh and drove off in the direction of Apple Hill, from which he had come.

"Merry Christmas!" Mother, Father, Alva, Meg, and

Betsy called out to him. They stood on the landing until the sound of the bells died away. Then Father and Alva took the sack between them and carried it into the house.

Christmas Eve had been a very long day, but it finally came to an end. The candles had burned down, the presents had been distributed, everyone had eaten nuts, apples, and butterscotch, and nobody had the energy to dance around the Christmas tree any more. Then Meg suddenly put her hands over her face and cried as if her heart would break. "Oh, Mother, now it's over, it's all over!"

But by the time she was tucked cosily into bed with her Christmas presents around her, she was already looking forward to the next day, when she was going to read her new books and try out her new skis and play with her new doll, who was called Kajsa. Betsy had a new doll too, a sailor doll that she had christened Albert.

She took Albert to bed with her and said to him, "Now, you be a good little boy." She was quiet for a while and then said slowly, "Even though I'm a house-owner and a property-owner, there wasn't any Christmas present for Albert. But next year," said Betsy, and stroked Albert gently on the head, "you're going to get a whole sackful—if I have any cash!"

CHAPTER VIII

Joseph in the Well

Winter would soon be gone, spring would soon be here, and Meg and Betsy tried to help it along. The ground was already bare in sunny spots, but on the north side of the house there were still some snowdrifts left, which bothered the girls. They attacked them with shovels and melted the snow in a barrel outside the kitchen door.

And that made spring come, all of a sudden. Fuzzy little bluebell buds shot up everywhere under the birch trees. Meg and Betsy got down on their knees every day to watch them grow.

There were tenants in the bird houses that Father had put up around June Hill, and every morning Meg and Betsy woke up to the sound of their singing. The river was so swollen that it washed over the landing. Meg and Betsy weren't allowed to go down there at all, so they played hopscotch on the garden path and threw balls against the woodshed wall. But Meg didn't have time to jump and play ball all the time. She had quite a lot of homework now and had to read and write and do arithmetic in the afternoon, sometimes for a whole hour. She thought that was far too much time to waste on homework. She could read extremely well, but spelling was harder, and arithmetic was the worst of all.

Sometimes Meg stayed in the kitchen with Alva to do her homework, and Betsy sat in the woodbin and pretended that she was Alva cleaning fish. She scraped the firewood with a kitchen knife so that the bark flew all over the place, and muttered about the scaly fish, just as she had heard Alva do. "Ha, how I hate fish! If I were doing the buying, there wouldn't *be* any fish."

Betsy had a good time and felt sorry for Meg having to sit there and struggle with those problems. Arithmetic must be very hard. Sometimes Father tried to make Meg practice adding in her head, so that she would become very good at it. Betsy too wanted Meg to be smart, and she thought of the cleverest arithmetic problems for her, just the way Father did.

"Meg," she said one day, "if there are ten boys and they take out one's appendix, how many are left?"

Meg wasn't the least bit grateful for the help and snorted. "Be quiet. Can't you see that I'm working on my problems?"

Alva laughed. She approved of Betsy's attempts to teach Meg arithmetic and gave her a problem of her own. "If I were to lay seventeen eggs here on the table and then took away five—" she began, but Meg roared with laughter.

"Can you lay eggs? Then why do we have to buy them from Apple Hill?"

Betsy laughed so hard that she cried. "Ha, ha, Alva can lay eggs! Now we don't have to buy any at Apple Hill. I'm going to tell Mother."

They went on teasing Alva and asked her to lay lots of eggs because it would soon be Easter.

Alva didn't give Meg any more arithmetic problems after that. Instead, she asked her questions about the Bible. There Meg did very well because Ida had told her so many Bible stories, and at school it was almost Meg's best subject.

But Ida didn't seem to have told her everything. One day, shortly before Easter, Meg came home from school in tears and threw her arms around her mother's neck. "Mother," she cried, "if you only knew how mean they were to Joseph!"

It took Mother a while to realize that it was Joseph in the Bible that Meg was talking about, because Meg was sobbing so. To think there could be people as mean as Joseph's brothers! To throw their own brother in a well and to sell him for a slave, and then to go home and tell his poor father that Joseph had been eaten by a wild animal!

"Yes, but afterward everything worked out well for Joseph," said Mother, trying to console her. "And don't you remember? He did see his father again."

Meg knew that, but it didn't improve matters. All day long she grieved over Joseph, and not until bedtime had she calmed down sufficiently to tell Betsy about him.

"Imagine, Betsy, selling your own brother as a slave!"

"What *is* a slave?" asked Betsy.

"A slave is someone who just works and works and works," said Meg.

"Is Father a slave?" Betsy wanted to know.

"Of course he isn't!"

"But he works and works and works," said Betsy.

"You don't understand anything," said Meg. "A slave is beaten with a whip. If he doesn't want to work, they beat him."

"I could borrow a whip from Apple Hill and beat Father just a little. Then he will be a slave," said Betsy, who thought that slaves sounded very interesting. She fell asleep almost at once, but Meg lay awake for a long time, thinking about Joseph being sold as a slave by his brothers.

Then Easter came, and Easter lilies, narcissuses, and crocuses were in bloom, and around June Hill the birches sprouted small green leaves, and Meg had spring vacation. Maja came from Apple Hill to bring lots of eggs—five dozen —because Alva stubbornly refused to lay any. Meg and Betsy began to think that Easter was almost as much fun as Christmas.

It was wonderful to eat red and blue and green eggs instead of just plain white ones. And it was fun to receive Easter cards. Grandmother and their cousins sent them pretty cards with downy chicks and lovely Easter lilies. But best of all, of course, was the Easter bunny, who came during the night when everyone was asleep and left small marzipan eggs in the grass on the lawn. That year he had invented something else. He laid two packages under the weeping willow tree, one labeled "To Meg," and the other "To Betsy." There was a little chocolate boy in each, and Meg and Betsy had never seen anything so charming.

Meg christened her chocolate boy Perker, and Betsy christened hers Smerker. During the whole Easter vacation they played with Perker and Smerker without licking them even once.

"I'm going to save Perker as long as I live," said Meg. "I'm never going to eat him up."

"And I'm going to save Smerker," said Betsy, "as long as I can."

Two days after Easter, Betsy was alone in the children's room for quite a long time. Meg was playing rummy in the kitchen with Alva when suddenly Betsy walked in with chocolate all over her face.

"I've eaten up Smerker," she said calmly.

Meg cried, "How could you do such a thing! You've eaten up your own child."

Betsy nodded. "Yes, just like the big pig at Apple Hill. She ate her children, remember? All nine piglets."

Meg thought Betsy was disgusting. "You are not the pig at Apple Hill. And you shouldn't act like a pig."

"Nobody should," said Betsy in the tone Alva sometimes used. "But the deed is done," she added with a nod, and obviously didn't regret it at all.

But the next morning, when she saw Meg sitting up in

her bed playing with Perker, Betsy began to feel pangs of regret—not so much that Smerker was gone, but that Perker was left.

"Meggie," she said slyly, "eat up Perker!"

Meg shook her head. "Never! Not ever."

She made a bed for Perker in a cigar box, with a cotton strip to lie on and a piece of blue satin for a quilt. Meg was having such a good time that Betsy was more and more remorseful, and finally she put her head on one side and begged, "Won't you let me borrow Perker—just once?"

"No," said Meg. "Not once."

"How many times, then?" asked Betsy.

"Not a single time, so there," Meg answered, "because you didn't have to eat Smerker." She tucked Perker into bed, laid the satin cover over him, and put him into the doll house.

Easter vacation was over, Meg was back at school again, and Betsy reigned alone over the children's room all morning.

One day when Meg came home and looked under the satin quilt in the cigar box in the doll house, Perker was gone. All that was there was a miserable little chocolate body without a head.

A scream rang through the house. Mother rushed in, terrified, thinking that Meg's life was in danger. But Meg just lay on her bed, screaming at the top of her lungs. "Betsy has bitten the head off Perker. Oh! Oh! Oh!"

Betsy was in the garden with Sasso. Mother called her in

and asked her severely, "Did you bite Perker's head off?"

Betsy looked to the right and she looked to the left. Then she looked straight ahead and said, "Maybe. I forget."

Meg screamed louder than ever, and Mother scolded Betsy for a long time. Then she said, "Tell Meg you're sorry."

Betsy stood still and didn't say a word.

"Well?" said Mother.

"What did you say?" asked Betsy.

"You have to ask Meg to forgive you."

"Ab-so-lute-ly not," said Betsy and pinched her mouth together the way she always did when she was being stubborn.

Mother tried to make her understand the seriousness of what she had done. Betsy certainly understood. But she would not say she was sorry. Meg didn't care, because it wouldn't put Perker's head back on.

Meg cried for a while, then sadly ate what was left of Perker. Betsy, beside her, begged shamelessly, "Can't you give me a little piece?"

"You horrid person!" said Meg. But she wasn't stingy, and Betsy got one of Perker's legs. Then they went outside to play together.

"Shall we look at the birds' nest?" asked Meg, and Betsy agreed. The nest was in an apple tree in the Nilssons' yard. Albert had shown it to them.

Meg and Betsy looked at the dear little pale blue eggs for a while, but they didn't touch them.

Under the apple tree was the Nilssons' old well. It was

empty and dry. Meg lifted up the broken cover and peered down, and just then she got one of her ideas.

"I know what we can do," she said. "We can play Joseph in the well."

Betsy clapped her hands. "And can I be Joseph?"

Meg considered for a minute. She would have liked to be Joseph herself, but she realized that Betsy couldn't manage the parts of the slave-dealer and Joseph's nasty brothers at the same time.

"I guess so," she said and went to get a small ladder from the Nilssons' laundry. She lowered it into the well so Betsy could climb down. The well wasn't deep, and Betsy wasn't at all afraid; in fact she was delighted with the adventure. This was going to be fun.

Meg pulled up the ladder and sat on the edge of the well, looking down at Betsy. It wasn't Betsy she saw, though, but poor Joseph, who was going to be sold as a slave to a strange land. Oh, how sorry she felt for him! But now she had to be Joseph's nasty brothers, so she said, "Nuts to you, Joseph. I'm going to sell you to the first slave-dealer who comes by. And that will serve you right."

Betsy joined in the game. "Ha, ha, then Father will beat you up when you get home."

"That's what you think," said Meg. "We'll just tell him you've been eaten up by a wild animal, so there!" She shuddered as she said it, but if she was Joseph's mean brothers, she had to play the part properly.

Then Betsy said, "Didn't Joseph get anything to eat at all when he was down in that well?"

"I don't know. Maybe," said Meg.

Actually it was a good idea of Betsy's. It would be fun to sit on the edge of the well and throw down food to Joseph. So Meg said, "Wait here, Betsy, and I'll run and get you a sandwich."

Betsy had to wait, whether she wanted to or not. She couldn't get out of the well without the ladder. First Meg went to the pantry and made a salami sandwich for Betsy and one for herself. Then she ran up to their room and got a pencil and a piece of cardboard and printed on the cardboard in big letters, "Little pretty slave for sale."

Then her eye lit on the empty cigar box standing on the table next to her bed, and she remembered what fun it had been when there was a little chocolate boy in it. Now he wasn't there any more, and it was that stupid Betsy's fault. Meg's anger suddenly flared up again. She hadn't forgiven Betsy at all, and she knew it. She was still furious when she got back to the well. Betsy didn't know that, but thought it was Joseph's nasty brothers coming back, and she was quite rude to them.

"Am I supposed to stay here in the well until I die, and not get anything to eat?" she snarled.

That made Meg still more furious. She wasn't playing now, and Betsy seemed greedier than the pig at Apple Hill.

"You can just sit there until you say you're sorry for bit-ing off Perker's head," Meg snapped.

Betsy looked up at her from the depths of the well, deeply hurt. Here she sat, being Joseph, who had never bitten off the head of a chocolate boy, and then Meg came, talking such nonsense.

"Little beast," muttered Meg, looking at the piece of card-board in her hand. "Little pretty slave for sale."

"I'll really sell you as a slave," said Meg, "just the way they did with Joseph. Then maybe you'll say you're sorry."

"Ab-so-lute-ly not," said Betsy and pinched her mouth to-gether.

Her stubbornness infuriated Meg. "Then you can just stay there," she said, throwing the salami sandwich down to Betsy. "You'd better eat now, because when you're a slave you'll never get anything to eat. You can be sure of that."

Betsy howled, but never would she ask to be forgiven. Meg waited for a while to see if Betsy would change her mind, but Betsy remained as stubborn as ever. She cried, but she didn't give in. Then Meg poked a little stick through the cardboard and set the sign in the grass near the well, with its terrible offer: "Little pretty slave for sale." Every slave-dealer who passed by would see it.

"Well, you've only yourself to blame," said Meg and went away to get beyond the sound of Betsy's frantic screams.

She wandered down to the river, eating her sandwich. The

water had gone down, and on the landing she saw her fishing rod. She put a little piece of sausage on the hook and sat down to fish. The river was full of small perch, but they didn't seem to like sausage. Anyway, they didn't bite. But it was fun just the same, and Meg completely forgot about Betsy for a while. When she finally remembered her, she was filled with remorse. All her fury was gone, and she dropped the fishing rod and rushed back to the well as fast as she could go. From a distance she began to call, "Betsy, I'm coming. Don't be frightened."

There was no answer, only a strange silence, no howling and no screaming—*and no Betsy!* She was gone. The well was empty. The sign was still there on its little stick, but something had been added with a pencil.

"Little pretty slave for sale. *This slave I have bought for five cents. Isidore, Turk and Slave-Dealer.*"

Poor Meg! If only she could sink into the ground and never come up again. What had she done? "Oh God," she prayed, "don't let it be true!" She had sold her own sister as a slave! There was a five-cent piece lying on the edge of the well. She was worse than Joseph's brothers, because they at least got a good price for him. Five cents—only enough to buy a few miserable pieces of butterscotch or five cookies. All of Betsy for a miserable five-cent piece! Meg moaned. Oh, what *had* she done? Oh, poor, poor Betsy! She had only wanted to frighten her a little. Who would have believed that a slave-dealer would come so soon—but those wicked creatures could probably smell a little slave for sale a long way off.

Meg sat on the edge of the well, imagining the most terrible things. The slave-dealer must have come along and wanted Betsy to work, but of course Betsy would say, "Ab-so-lute-ly not," and then he'd take his whip out. Oh, poor Betsy! And poor miserable Meg who had sold her! And poor Mother and Father! They'd lost both their girls at once, because Meg could never go home and tell them she had sold Betsy—and to a slave-dealer—for five cents. Never, never in a million years! Now she'd have to go off into the woods and live the life of an outlaw, like Robin Hood.

There lay the horrible five-cent piece on the edge of the well. With a whimper Meg picked it up and threw it into the hole. Then she rushed sobbing out through the gate. She must flee to the woods before they found out the terrible thing that had happened. But something stopped her. Soon it would be dark, and how would she dare to be alone in the woods? Wasn't there some safe place for a person who has sold her sister into slavery? Maybe Ida. Ida was so kind. Maybe she would hide Meg and let her lie on the floor like a dog and only eat bread crusts—anything would be better than having to live the life of an outlaw in the woods. Yes, Ida was her only hope.

Ida was startled when Meg rushed in, sobbing wildly. "Oh,

dear, dear, you're running as if you had the police after you."

Meg looked at her in horror. The police, Ida said. Of course selling slaves must be a crime, and the police would come and take her when they found out what she had done! With a sob Meg threw herself on the floor and put her arms around Ida's legs.

"Please, please, Ida, please let me lie on your floor and just eat bread crusts."

"Eat bread crusts—why, in heaven's name?" asked Ida, puzzled. "Poor little thing, what's wrong? Has something terrible happened at June Hill?"

Something terrible at June Hill! Meg sobbed as if her heart would break. Oh, if Ida only knew! Then she would understand that there could never again be anything but unhappiness at June Hill.

"Tell me what is the matter," said Ida.

But Meg was so terribly ashamed about her slave trade that she couldn't bring herself to tell. After a lot of coaxing, Ida did get her to say that something so terrible had happened that Meg could never go back home. Ida shook her head in a worried way.

"Dear, dear, whatever it is you've done, you don't have to lie on the floor and eat bread crusts." She lifted Meg onto her bed and wrapped a blanket around her.

"Just sleep for a while," she said, "and you'll feel better."

The words were hardly out of her mouth when Meg was asleep. Slave-trading is exhausting work. She lay there completely worn out, her face streaked with tears and her eyelashes dark against her cheek.

"You poor little thing," murmured Ida. "Sleep, and I'll go over to June Hill and find out what is wrong."

Meg slept for a while, then woke up with a start. At first she didn't know where she was, but when she looked around and saw Ida's favorite picture, of a mountain spitting fire, on the wall above the bed, she remembered. Oh, why did she have to wake up again? And where was Ida? A dreadful suspicion flashed into Meg's mind. Maybe Ida had gone for the police! Perhaps it was against the law to hide criminals. Ida was a good soul, but she probably didn't want to go to jail even for Meg's sake. She must have gone for the police.

Meg heard steps in the hall, and she heard Ida talking to someone. Now they were coming to get her. "Just come right in," said Ida.

With puffy eyes Meg stared toward the door. "Help, Mother, help!" she breathed. But she could never expect help from Mother, nor from Father, either—she who had sold their Betsy as a slave. The police could come and get her any time—and here they were.

The door opened, and someone was standing there, not a big policeman, but a little person—Betsy! Meg stared as if she were seeing a ghost. Oh, Betsy, could it really be true? With a sob Meg stretched out her hands. She wanted to touch Betsy to be sure she was really there. She wanted to hug her. She was terribly fond of Betsy.

Filled with love and remorse, Meg opened her arms, and Betsy ran right toward her. But when she reached Meg she gave her a good push. "Move over. I want to look at the mountain on fire too. You've had your turn."

Betsy clambered up onto the bed and knelt to look at the mountain spitting fire. But Meg looked only at Betsy.

"Did you run away from the slave-dealer?" she asked, full of shame and at the same time full of admiration. What a brave and enterprising little sister she had!

"What slave-dealer?" asked Betsy. "We're not playing that game any more. Albert gave me pretzels and he didn't give you any."

Meg stared at her. "Albert! Was it Albert who got you out of the well?"

Betsy went on staring at the flaming mountain and paid no attention to what Meg was saying. "That's the best picture I've ever seen in my whole life," she said.

"Was it Albert?" Meg insisted.

"Yes, of course, and he gave me pretzels too."

"Yes, I know that," said Meg. "You are a good girl, Betsy, but that Albert is a skunk."

Darkness had fallen over June Hill, and the red house by the river was asleep. The sun had gone down and big dark blue shadows lingered among the birches, which looked their most beautiful in their green gossamer veils under the cool, clear spring sky. The narcissus, gleaming white in the darkness, gave off a most delicious fragrance. Earlier in the evening the air had resounded with birdsong, but now all the little birds were sleeping. All was still.

But no, not quite. In the red house voices were singing:

"Oh, how lovely is the evening,
Is the evening,
When the bells are sweetly ringing. . . ."

If you stood below the window of the children's room, you could hear it. And someone was there, listening. A thin boy with shaggy blond hair was standing in the shadow of the weeping willow tree. He stood there quietly, listening as he had listened so many nights before. Albert liked to hear people sing. No one knew he was there, and soon he would disappear, tiptoeing very carefully because he didn't want to step on the narcissus. The Right Honorable Albert, Turk and Slave-Dealer, was a very good boy.

"Oh, how lovely is the evening,
When the bells are sweetly ringing. . . ."

Betsy went on singing, although Mother and Father had already said good night and closed the door. But she stopped suddenly.

"Meggie," she said, "may I lie in your bed?"

"Yes, you may," said Meg. And cold little feet tiptoed across the floor to Meg's bed.

"May I sleep in your arms?" asked Betsy.

"Of course." Oh, everything was perfect! Meg was so happy that Betsy was her sister and was lying there, safe at home and not in some miserable slave-dealer's power.

Meg hugged Betsy tight. "Betsy, you must never, never leave me."

"No, I'll never go away, not ever," Betsy assured her. "The main thing is for you and me to be together all the time."

Outside, the spring sky was darkening. Darkness had crept into every corner of the children's room, but Meg thought it was a friendly darkness. It was their own familiar, comfortable darkness, hers and Betsy's.

"Meggie," said Betsy, and put her cold little feet against Meg's warm ones. "Meggie, tell me more about ghosts and robbers."